MOMENT OF TRUTH

Clint started to rein Duke away, but the big man grabbed Duke's bridle. "Hang on, mister," the man said, his voice taking on a low and nasty tone. "We just gave you and that pretty lady of yours a friendly invitation to share our company and now you're telling us that we aren't good enough for you?"

Clint knew that he was in a fix with the big man hanging on Duke's bridle, and so he decided to give talk one last chance before he went for his six-gun. "I sure didn't mean to insult you, mister, but me and the lady will be riding on. So I'm asking you to let go of my bridle."

The big man's eyes widened in mock concern. "And what'll happen if I don't?"

Clint knew that there was no sense in further conversation. His hand flashed to his six-gun, and it came up so fast that no one was prepared for the move.

Clint asked in a quiet voice, "You want a hole blown in the top of your fat skull, or would you rather let go of my bridle?"

DON'T MISS THESE
ALL-ACTION WESTERN SERIES
FROM THE BERKLEY PUBLISHING GROUP

THE GUNSMITH by J. R. Roberts
> Clint Adams was a legend among lawmen, outlaws, and
> ladies. They called him . . . the Gunsmith.

LONGARM by Tabor Evans
> The popular long-running series about U.S. Deputy
> Marshal Long—his life, his loves, his fight for justice.

LONE STAR by Wesley Ellis
> The blazing adventures of Jessica Starbuck and the martial
> arts master, Ki. Over eight million copies in print.

SLOCUM by Jake Logan
> Today's longest-running action Western. John Slocum rides
> a deadly trail of hot blood and cold steel.

THE GUNSMITH

149

SPANISH GOLD

J. R. ROBERTS

JOVE BOOKS, NEW YORK

SPANISH GOLD

A Jove Book / published by arrangement with
the author

PRINTING HISTORY
Jove edition / May 1994

ISBN: 0-515-11377-8

A JOVE BOOK®
Jove Books are published by The Berkley Publishing Group,
200 Madison Avenue,
New York, New York 10016.
JOVE and the "J" design are trademarks
belonging to Jove Publications, Inc.

PRINTED IN THE UNITED STATES OF AMERICA

10 9 8 7 6 5 4 3 2 1

THE GUNSMITH

149

SPANISH GOLD

ONE

"Hot damn!" Clint Adams cried out as a huge speckled trout took his bait and bent his willow pole almost double.

Clint had been dozing along the banks of the Gila River, but now he was fully awake. Jumping to his feet, he began to play with the trout, testing its strength against his skill with a crude pole and twenty feet of flyweight line.

"Come on! Fight!" the Gunsmith shouted happily. "Show me your stuff!"

As if understanding the challenge, the huge trout spun from the water and flashed in the sun like a silver coin. Shaking and twisting, it splashed back into the current and dove for a nearby fallen and half-submerged tree.

"No!" Clint bellowed with dismay as he staggered upriver, trying to keep the monster from snapping his flimsy line. "Get away from there!"

But the big trout was in the air again, sunfishing against the New Mexico pines. Clint stepped on a

1

mossy rock and lost his footing. He crashed into the river, willow pole still firmly locked in his fists. The damage, however, was already done. The trout had reached the underside of the tree and its fins had propelled it through a maze of branches.

"Dammit!" the Gunsmith roared, pulling on the line but feeling no give. The line was hopelessly snagged.

The Gunsmith dropped the willow pole and glared at the fallen cottonwood. He now had to either give up the fish and let it suffer a slow death with a hook in its mouth, or try to capture the damned thing by crawling out on the fallen tree and attempting to reel the fish in with his bare hands.

Clint chose the riskier course of action. He removed his boots and gun belt, stowed them neatly at the foot of a big rock, then began to inch his way out to a place that appeared to be just above the snagged trout. It was a dicey piece of work because the half-submerged cottonwood was as slick as calf slobber. Further complicating things were dozens of sharp, prong-like branches sticking out of the tree's trunk; all of them seemed determined to impede the Gunsmith's forward progress.

Ten feet out, he was ready to say to hell with it, but just then the snagged trout darted to the surface and began to splash. The trout was magnificent, and the Gunsmith's mouth almost watered to think about how sweet and juicy its flesh would be after a few minutes in his frying pan.

"He's got to be at least two feet long!" Clint said with a wide grin.

The fish was tantalizingly close. It kept splashing and fighting on the fishing line. Clint could see its beady eyes rolling and its mouth opening and closing as if that might also help free it from the annoying metal barb embedded in its upper lip.

"Another two yards," Clint muttered, trying to snake around a particularly thick and bothersome branch.

As he stretched, the mossy log shifted a little under his weight and the strong river current. Just another few feet and . . . "Ahhhh!"

The cottonwood broke from its mooring and rolled. Clint thrust a hand at the snagged trout, but it panicked and the hook was torn from its mouth. The trout dove for the river's bottom as the tree and the Gunsmith rolled forward.

Clint tried to throw himself out of harm's way from the massive and now floating tree. But one of its branches hooked him in the lower back and jammed him deep underwater. Pure terror gripped the Gunsmith as he struggled to free himself but could not. The branch was tangled in his pants, and only a final shred of reason told him to unbutton the pants and rip them from his body.

When the Gunsmith was at last able to claw to the surface, he sucked in fresh air, filling his aching lungs, then swam for all his might in order to outrace the churning cottonwood. It wasn't until Clint was nearly fifty yards out in front of the floating tree that he dared to angle toward the safety of shore. The Gila River was swift in these Mogollon Mountains of western New Mexico as it plunged toward the lower desert elevations of Arizona. It was all that the Gunsmith could do to thrash his way back to the shore, far below where he'd first entered the water. By the time he managed to drag himself up onto the riverbank, he was badly winded.

Clint lay panting and wheezing in his underwear on the sandy riverbank for nearly a quarter of an hour. He knew that he was damned lucky to still be alive and was furious at himself for risking his life to catch a stupid fish. Clint realized full well that had he not been able to remove his pants quickly enough, or had another broken and submerged branch impaled him, he'd have died in the kind of freakish accident that often happened in the wilderness.

"No more fishing pole, line, hook, and no more damned fishing today," he muttered at the azure New Mexico sky that hung like a pale blue shroud over the Mogollon Mountains.

The Gunsmith was just about to climb to his feet when he heard a scream. It caused him to jump up, and it was then that he realized his gun was several hundred yards upriver.

"Help!" the cry echoed again.

Clint jerked his head this way and that, trying to get a bearing on the cry for help. It seemed to him that the cry was coming from upriver, hopefully beyond where he'd left his boots and gun belt.

Hurrying forward, the Gunsmith winced and grunted with pain as his tender feet were bruised by sharp rocks.

"No!" a man's voice screamed as a gunshot echoed up and down the rocky mountain canyon.

Clint gritted his teeth and began to run toward his boots and holstered six-gun. It sounded as if someone had just been executed.

"Hold it!" a voice from the nearby trees ordered. "Mister, stop or I'll blow a hole in you bigger than a Confederate cannonball."

The Gunsmith skidded to a halt as a man leapt out of the forest with a shotgun.

"Throw up your hands!"

Clint raised his hands and tried to manufacture an innocent smile, but he was seething inside. First he'd been stupid enough to almost get himself drowned, now he was standing unarmed and half-naked before a killer with a shotgun in his fists and murder in his eyes.

"Don't shoot," Clint called.

"Where the hell are your pants and boots?"

Clint realized that this man who had him under guard could not possibly see his holstered gun and boots. And although the soles of the Gunsmith's bare feet were already cut, bruised, and throbbing, it was his pistol rather than his boots that he most desired.

"I lost them when I fell in the river."

"Jesus!" the bearded man snorted with disgust. "I never heard of the likes of you. I'll bet you're workin' with the one we just shot. I'll just bet anything you know where we can find that Spanish gold."

"No," Clint said quickly. "I'm alone, and I don't know about any Spanish gold."

"What the hell *are* you doin' up here?"

"Fishing."

"Fishing!" the bearded man exclaimed. "Why, sure you are! Everybody fishes half-naked with no pole or line. You ain't no damn fisherman, you're in cahoots with Abe Morton!"

The Gunsmith wagged his head back and forth. He started to argue, but just then a second man stepped out of the trees, holding a pistol. When he saw Clint, he paused. "Your friend Abe is dyin'. We're going to shoot you too, if you don't tell us where that Spanish gold is hidden."

"What Spanish gold?"

"Deke, why don't we just blow a hole in his belly and be done with it?"

"But if I do that," Deke said, "how are we going to find out where all that gold is buried? Dammit, you went and killed Abe before we could get him to talk."

"That's right," the Gunsmith said, trying to buy precious time, "if you shoot me now, how are you going to find out about that Spanish gold?"

"So," Deke shouted in triumph, "you *do* know where that gold is buried!"

"I have a pretty fair idea," Clint said, deciding that he was a dead man if he didn't appeal to their greed.

"What does that mean?" the man with the pistol asked. "Either you know where the Spanish gold is buried and you're going to take us there, or you don't know and we're going to shoot your guts clean out. Now, which is it?"

"I know!"

"Good," Deke said. "You got any pants at your camp?"

The man with the pistol barked a cruel laugh. "Maybe this fella just likes to run around half-nekked!"

"I've got an extra pair of pants and some moccasins at my camp," Clint said, flushing with anger and embarrassment. "And I need them if I'm going to help you find that Spanish gold. But there's another thing too."

"What's that?"

"Abe Morton."

"Forget about that old man! He was as stubborn as a mule. Maybe you'll show a little more sense and take us to that Spanish gold."

Clint knew that there was no backing out now, if he was to save his hide. "Yeah. But Abe was my friend, and I mean to see he gets a proper burial."

"To hell with him!" Deke shouted.

"I need to ask him some questions before he dies."

"How come?"

"He knows the trail to that Spanish gold better than I do," Clint argued, making up his story as he went. "I'm not even sure that I can find it without getting a few more details out of him."

"You mean you never even been there?"

Clint swallowed. "No," he said, "I was going to help Abe uncover the treasure. We were on our way, but he didn't trust me completely. I have a good idea where the gold is buried, but I need some details. Maybe even a map."

"Abe is dying!"

"Then I'd better have a talk with him right now," Clint said, deciding that he had no choice but to gamble. "Because, if he can't talk, I may not be able to find the buried Spanish treasure."

The two men exchanged glances, and the one with the shotgun finally nodded. "All right, if Abe is still alive, he can talk to all of us together. Come along and don't try any funny business. This double-barreled shotgun will spread your guts all over creation."

Clint knew there was no chance that he would be able to make a break for freedom and collect his gun, not with the way he was being guarded. So he followed orders and was led into the forest.

The moment he saw Abe Morton, Clint knew that the old prospector had suffered a fatal gunshot to the chest. Abe had also been severely beaten. His nose had been broken, his lips smashed, and his teeth knocked out. One of his eyes was swollen shut. There was blood caked in his right ear, telling the Gunsmith that the poor man had suffered a concussion even before he'd tried to escape.

"Abe was one tough old son of a bitch," Deke said with an unmistakable trace of admiration. "We beat him bloody for three days, and he still wouldn't tell us where the Spanish gold was hidden."

"How did you find out about it in the first place?"

"Abe would go to Silver City, and he'd drink a bit. Also, the fool spent some Spanish coins the last time he visited Santa Fe. Why, everyone knew he'd stumbled on a fortune. And then we found his map."

"You did?"

"Sure." Deke patted his chest. "Got it right here in my pocket!"

"Then why . . ."

"Part of the map is missin'!" Deke spat. "Abe musta tore it in half and then burned the most important part that shows exactly where the damn gold is buried."

Clint nodded, the situation suddenly becoming very clear to him. "Abe?" he said, touching the dying man's battered face. "Abe, can you hear me? It's your friend, Clint."

Abe's eyelids fluttered and he tried to speak, but his voice sounded like a rusty hinge. The Gunsmith looked sideways at the two men who had their weapons trained on him. "Deke, maybe a sip of water would help Abe talk."

"Henry, get your canteen," Deke ordered his partner. "And dammit, I sure wish that you hadn't shot Abe. It's a lucky thing that we chanced upon his partner or we'd be shit out of luck and never find the gold."

Henry flushed with anger. "You saw him! The crazy old fool wouldn't stop runnin'. You're too gimped up to run, and he was getting away from us. I yelled at him to stop, but he wouldn't. So what else was I supposed to do?"

"Dammit, you said he was so weak and old that you could catch him on foot!"

"He turned out to be a lot faster than I figured," Henry admitted. "I thought he was going to get to the river and jump in and then maybe he'd get away. There was no choice but to drop him with a bullet."

"You should have aimed for his legs," Deke spat. "Now get your canteen."

When Henry disappeared into the trees, the Gunsmith thought maybe he could make a lunge for Deke, but the man backed up and cocked the hammer of his shotgun in warning. "Don't even think about trying it."

Clint took the man's advice. Maybe with a pistol Deke would have rushed his shot and missed, but there was no chance of that happening with the shotgun.

"Abe," Clint said, leaning close to the dying prospector. "You've got to help me find that Spanish gold."

Clint glanced over at Deke. He would have given anything to have spoken with the old prospector alone for a few minutes, but that was clearly out of the question. He turned back to the dying man and could not help feeling a flush of outrage at the beating Abe Morton had endured at the hands of these two heartless bastards.

Abe stared up at Clint through his one open eye and his lips moved. Clint leaned forward, barely able to hear the old man's raspy whisperings.

"Mrs. Annie Bates," he wheezed. "Daughter in Silver City. Tell her . . ." Abe began to cough blood. His face grew very pale, and he struggled to breathe.

"Easy," Clint urged, "just take it real easy."

"Here!" Henry said, thrusting the canteen at the Gunsmith. "If you don't know exactly where that Spanish gold is buried, you damn sure had better get Abe to talk before he dies or you'll be joining him in hell today."

The Gunsmith's head snapped back, and he was reckless with rage. "You bastards had no right to beat an old man half to death and then shoot him down like this!"

Henry stepped forward, and his fist crashed into the Gunsmith's jaw, knocking him over. He reared back and booted Clint in the ribs.

"Ugggh," Clint gasped, as a sheet of crimson passed behind his eyes and he tried to protect himself from another kick.

Henry would have booted him in the face, but Deke jumped in between them.

"Enough!" Deke shouted, knocking the smaller man aside and raising his shotgun. "Henry, you're a fool. You already killed the old man and now you're trying to kill this fella. For once, use your goddamn head and think! We need this man alive or we can forget about finding that Spanish gold."

"I don't think he knows where it's buried," Henry snarled, eyes blazing with hatred.

"Sure he does! The old man hired him to help dig up all that buried Spanish treasure. And if he dies too, we're at a dead end."

Henry's face was contorted with rage; he looked like he did not care about anything except kicking the life out of the Gunsmith.

"Henry," Deke said with quiet menace, "I need him alive more than I need you alive."

Henry blinked as the meaning of Deke's words hit home. "All right," he choked. "But I don't trust this son of a bitch, and I ain't even sure that he knows where Abe's cache of Spanish gold is buried."

"That may be true," Deke said, glancing down at the Gunsmith. "If it is, we'll make him curse the day he was born. I'm betting this fella will sing like a bird. Don't forget, I know some Apache torture."

"You mean like wet rawhide around his balls?"

"Or his head . . . or both," Deke said with an almost demented laugh that sent chills up and down Clint's spine.

When the Gunsmith looked at his captors, he saw no trace of humanity in their dark eyes. They were brutish men who did not even know the meaning of the word mercy.

They had no more compassion than a pair of starving wolves.

TWO

"Can you hear me?" Clint asked, leaning close to the dying man. "Abe?"

"Ask him if he hid the other part of that damned treasure map!" Deke growled.

"Abe," Clint said, taking the dying man's hand, "I'm going to try and help you."

Abe opened his one good eye and stared at the Gunsmith for so long he thought the man might have already died. But then Abe's mashed lips quivered and he whispered, "Cibola."

"Hear that?" Henry shouted.

"I heard," Clint said.

"He's talkin' about the Seven Lost Cities of Cibola!" Deke said. "They're legends, and they ain't never been found. Maybe he found the first one, and that's where he got those golden Spanish coins."

Clint leaned close to the dying prospector. "Is that true? Did you find a lost city of gold?"

"Yeah, but you'll never live to find it!"

The force and savagery of the dying man's voice startled the Gunsmith. "Listen," Clint said, "these fellas are gonna kill me if I don't help find that buried treasure. So anything you can tell me would . . ."

"Annie," Abe whispered.

"Why that old bastard is still callin' for his daughter in Silver City!" Henry snarled, lashing out with his boot and catching Abe Morton in the side.

Something exploded in the Gunsmith, and he grabbed Henry's boot and twisted the man to the earth. Before Deke could interfere, Clint smashed Henry twice, breaking his nose so that blood poured down Henry's face. He would have done a lot more damage except that Deke batted him across the head with the barrel of his shotgun. Stunned, Clint pulled back and jumped to his feet.

Henry's hand flew to his broken nose. A curse erupted from his lips and his hand dropped to his side arm.

"No!" Deke shouted at his enraged partner.

But Henry was crazy with rage. His gun started up, and he would have shot the Gunsmith except that one of Deke's shotgun barrels belched fire, lead, and smoke. A charge of shot struck Henry in the chest and lifted him completely off his feet. The man was propelled backward and slammed against a tree. He was dead before he slid down the tree's trunk and rolled over onto his deathbed of pine needles.

The Gunsmith spun around and would have jumped for Deke, but the bearded man took a step, back raised his shotgun, and said, "You ready to die right now, mister?"

Clint took a deep breath and calmed himself. Then he turned to look at Abe. "The old man's dead."

"Yeah," Deke said, "Henry finally killed him. And

then I had to finally kill Henry. Now the question is, am I going to have to kill you too—or are you going to take me to that buried Spanish gold?"

"And what if I do?" Clint demanded to know. "Then you kill me?"

"Maybe not. If there's enough gold, I'll give you some, and we can go our separate ways."

Clint didn't believe it. He knew that even if he somehow found the gold, he was finished. Deke would blow him apart and take all the gold.

"All right," Clint said, willing to buy himself a little time, "so we'll find the buried treasure."

"You can do that?"

Clint's mind raced to come up with a story that Deke would find believable. "Abe gave me the other half of his treasure map."

"Why?"

"So we'd have to trust each other. I couldn't find the gold without him, and he might not even have been able to find the gold without me."

"Let's see the second half and we'll match 'em together and get rich."

"I lost it in the river," Clint said with a shake of his head. "It was in my pants, and I had to cut them free or I'd have drowned. They got snagged by a log and were pulling me under."

"Then I guess that's the end of this story," Deke said, raising the shotgun.

"No!" Clint lowered his voice. "Listen, Deke. I memorized every detail of my half of the map. All I need is to get to the place where his map ended. There was a river—this Gila River—and a sheer cliff."

"There are hundreds of cliffs along this river."

"This one was bigger than most. It had trees hanging off its sides and . . . and a trail."

Deke studied him closely down the long barrel of his smoking shotgun. "What else did it have?"

Clint was gambling. If he could just have a day or two, he was sure that he could find a way to get the drop on Deke and save his life. But he needed time.

"It had a . . . big lightning-burned pine tree beside it, so there's no chance of mistaking it for any other place along this river."

Deke's shoulders relaxed. "You're sure?"

"Very sure. Like I said before, I haven't been there, but I studied the half of the treasure map that Abe gave me and put it to memory."

"So where is the gold buried?"

"Near the tree."

"How near?"

Clint knew that he could say no more. To give this man any more specifics would convince him that he could find the place alone. And yet, to refuse to say more might just cause Deke to kill him.

"It wasn't possible to tell exactly," Clint hedged.

"What the hell does that mean?"

"It means that there are a couple of other signs that I have to hunt for which were just not very clear on the map. That's all that I'm saying."

For several long moments, Deke seemed to waver with indecision about pulling the trigger. Finally, he lowered the shotgun and said, "Get down on your belly while I tie your hands behind your back. Time is wasting."

"I'd like to bury my friend."

"To hell with that stubborn old man."

Clint wanted to argue, but when Deke raised the shotgun to his shoulder again, he changed his mind.

Once the Gunsmith was led at the point of Deke's shotgun back to his camp, the man said, "Nice horse. Nice saddle and rifle too. I'll be taking your outfit and you can ride mine."

Clint shook his head. "That big, black gelding and I have been together over a lot of tough trails. I think it'd be better if you rode your own horse, Deke."

"When I want your opinion, I'll ask for it. I like the looks of that black gelding, and we might just as well get acquainted right now."

"Suit yourself," Clint said, knowing that Duke would not stand to be ridden by anyone other than himself. "I could break camp, pack up my gear, and be a whole lot more useful if you untied my wrists."

"I can break your camp," Deke said gruffly. "You just sit down on that rock and stay put. If you try to run, I'll catch and kill you. No man can run worth spit with his hands tied behind his back."

"I know that."

"Good!" Deke marched into the Gunsmith's camp. He started to pack and then he got distracted by Clint's food. In no time at all, he was feasting on sourdough bread, tinned sardines and peaches, then washing everything down with the whiskey he'd found in the Gunsmith's saddlebags.

"You eat real good, mister. What's your name?"

"Clint."

"Well, Clint," Deke said, stroking his full black beard and then wiping his lips with the back of his sleeve, "I want to let you know that I'd prefer to make things easy between us."

"Then untie me."

"Not *that* easy. What I'm saying is that I want to find that Spanish gold, split it up fair between us, then part company, not as friends, but as rich business associates."

"Business associates?"

"Yep."

"All right."

"You see," Deke continued, "what you may not know is that there are bound to be others comin' to find you and that dead old man. Abe wasn't very smart, what with all his bragging and spending those Spanish coins. Me and Henry just happened to find you fellas first, that's all."

"I'm beginning to understand," Clint said. "You're saying that we might have to fight off people trying to do to us what you and Henry did to Abe and me."

"Huh?"

"Never mind," Clint said. "I get your drift. We'll be needing to watch our back trail."

"You got that right."

"So what happens if we do get jumped?"

"If the odds are long, then I give you a gun and we try to stay alive long enough to claim that Spanish gold."

"I see."

"But until then," Deke said, "I'm keeping your hands tied behind your back and a close eye on you. To do otherwise would be stupid."

"I can see that you are not stupid."

"Damn right I'm not."

Clint leaned back on the rock and turned his face up to the sun. His clothes were already starting to dry, and he no longer felt chilled, although his ribs hurt like the devil where he had been kicked. The Gunsmith tried not to smile as he thought about what would happen when big Deke climbed on board the black gelding. Other men had tried to steal Duke and ride the gelding away. Every one of them had been bucked higher than a barn roof, and the Gunsmith saw no reason to suppose that Deke would fare any better.

"Let's get our horses and bring them over to camp and then we're ready to ride," Deke said, motioning Clint back toward the river.

A few minutes later, they had gathered up Deke's, Henry's, and Abe Morton's horses and outfits and led them back to Clint's camp.

"Mount up," Deke ordered.

"I can't as long as my hands are tied behind my back."

"Here," Deke said, leading his own horse over to a low rock. "Jump up on this rock, then onto my horse. Don't worry, he won't buck. He's as gentle as a milk cow."

"Good."

"What about your black gelding?"

"Duke is also as gentle as a milk cow."

Deke nodded with satisfaction. He walked over to the black gelding, and the horse rolled its eyes and snorted with alarm. "Hey!" Deke warned. "You behave or I'll spur the hell outta ya!"

But the moment Deke got his leg swinging over the Gunsmith's cantle, Duke exploded. Deke lasted only three jumps before he was propelled skyward. He did a complete somersault and landed on the back of his head.

By then the Gunsmith was already at the dazed man's side, managing to extract Deke's big hunting knife and cut the leather bonds that held his wrists together behind his back. He snatched Deke's six-gun from his holster and said, "New plans, Deke. I want the half of the map that you took from Abe before you killed him."

"Go to hell!"

Clint struck Deke across the side of his head with the gun. "I can find it myself."

The map was in Deke's coat pocket. It wasn't much, just a badly wrinkled piece of paper with a few names that were unfamiliar to the Gunsmith. "Are we as far as this map takes us?"

"Yeah," Deke said, holding his head. "That's why we jumped Abe here once we figured he knew we were on his trail and he wouldn't go no nearer to the gold unless we got rough."

"You miscalculated that old man's resolve," Clint said.

"His what?"

"His backbone," Clint explained. "Some men will fold under pressure or pain, others just harden. It seems to me that Abe was one of the latter kinds."

"He was a fool. We offered him a share, but he wanted it all. Said he'd hunted all his life for a find like this and he wasn't going to share it with the likes of us."

"Can you blame him?"

Deke looked away, and the Gunsmith said, "Roll over onto your stomach."

"I thought we was going to be partners."

"I'm taking you down to Silver City and handing you over to the sheriff."

"I didn't kill Abe Morton! Henry did!"

"Yeah, I know. But you were a part of it, and you'll go to prison, if not swing from a hangman's noose."

"Well, what about the Spanish gold we was going to find?"

"To hell with it," Clint snapped. "On your belly. Hands behind your back."

The Gunsmith tied Deke's wrists so tightly that his prisoner wailed and complained that he would lose feeling in his hands and his fingers might rot and fall off before they could get down to Silver City.

"I don't give a damn if both your hands fall off," Clint growled. "You beat an old man mercilessly, then hunted him down like a varmint and shot him in the lungs. Don't plead for any favors from me, Deke. I'm just hoping that you'll go to the gallows."

Deke's eyes radiated hatred. "I knew that I couldn't trust you."

"Well," Clint said, "at least you were right about something."

The Gunsmith draped the bodies over the spare horses. He lashed them down, covering them with their own bedrolls. Then he helped Deke onto his horse and gathered up his own reins. All the while, the bearded man glared at him in silence.

"Let's ride," Clint said, mounting Duke and picking up his reins.

"Did you teach that black son of a bitch to buck off strangers like that?"

"Nope. He just naturally hates a horse thief."

"I shoulda listened to you and stayed to my own horse. If I'd have done that, we'd be heading off to get rich instead of just me going to jail."

"Yep," Clint said, "it's just sad how life never quite works out the way we expect."

Deke scowled at him.

"Too bad," Clint said, without a trace of sympathy.

"You going after that Spanish gold?"

"Nope. Until you and Henry showed up, I'd never even heard of such a thing."

Deke's jaw dropped. "You mean . . ."

"Yeah," Clint said. "Until you showed up, I was interested in nothing more than catching fish and getting a good long rest."

"What about now?"

Clint thought about that. "After I deliver you to Silver City, I might look into this treasure business. Where does your trail to Cibola run cold?"

"Damned if I'll tell you anything!"

"Fine," Clint said. "I was a lawman once, and I'm pretty good at tracking down rumors. Maybe I'll just follow this one and see where it takes me."

"I hope that it takes you straight to hell."

Clint smiled. "You know, these rumors of lost cities of gold have been floating around for a couple of centuries. Francisco Coronado roamed all over the Southwest, and he never found anything but rock, sage, and unfriendly Indians."

"I saw them golden coins that Abe was spending in Santa Fe. I even saw a piece of Spanish armor that he was showing off."

"You did?" Clint asked with surprise.

"Yeah. It was all rusted and battered, but you could see that it was part of a helmet. Abe said that there was more where that came from."

Clint's mind soared with the possibilities. Always

before, he had heard stories of lost Spanish gold, especially from lonely, half-demented prospectors who had wandered so long in the deserts that their minds had taken to prolonged flights of fantasy. But now here was a man who had actually unearthed not only Spanish gold, but possibly a conquistador's armor.

"I hope it kills you," Deke snarled.

"What?"

"I hope that you go searching for that damned hidden gold and it kills you. It's said that them old buried treasures have a curse on 'em."

"If you believed that, you wouldn't have gone after it for yourselves."

"I ain't very superstitious, but I can see now that it's cursed because Henry is dead and I'll hang for certain if you get me to a judge or someone else searching for the Spanish gold doesn't just up and shoot us both."

"There are no guarantees." The Gunsmith looked away. He kept wondering if this trail to the Spanish gold had a beginning and an end. Who would know besides poor, dead Abe?

"Annie," Clint said, remembering the last word that Abe had uttered.

"What?" Deke asked.

"Nothing," Clint said. "I was just talking to myself."

THREE

Silver City rested at the knee of the Mogollon Mountains at an altitude of almost six thousand feet. Clint had always liked this wild West boomtown, and even though the silver mines were finally starting to decline, Silver City had the look and feel of a county seat that would survive. Cattle ranching had become more prominent, and Clint knew that a huge lumber mill was under construction. To make matters even better, a narrow-gauge railroad was being constructed northward from the Southern Pacific at Demming. There was even talk of building a university in Silver City, and the discovery of vast copper deposits had all of New Mexico buzzing with excitement.

"If we move right along," Clint said, "we can be there before midnight."

"To hell with that," Deke said, glancing up at the setting sun that glistened across a mantle of snowcapped mountains. "I say we make camp."

"What you say doesn't matter. We'll push on."

Deke muttered an obscenity, but the Gunsmith didn't
care. They were on a steep mountainside trail and, if
they hurried, they would be off it before darkness fell.
After that, they would come upon a mining road and
the last few miles would be dark, but easy going.

As he rode along leading the spare horses carrying
the bodies of Henry and Abe Morton, Clint could not
help but feel a sense of excitement about the prospect of finding a hidden fortune in Spanish gold. Sure,
like just about everyone else on the western frontier,
he'd been duped into chasing after lost treasure based
on some phony map. Treasure maps commonly sold
to the gullible, and you could even save money by
buying them in quantity. Some treasure maps were
elaborate hoaxes written on real parchment or leather
in order to look original. Other maps were obviously
reproductions, sometimes scribbled on paper but with
the admonition that they had been faithfully copied
from a "real" map. Abe's map fit this latter descrip-
tion.

The Gunsmith had heard all the stories of lost mines,
lost fortunes, and dying prospectors like Abe Morton
who had been murdered for information to their fortunes. Such stories were always interesting and fun to
think about. They offered hardworking men a chance
to fantasize for the price of a cheap but worthless map.
But *this* story somehow seemed to the Gunsmith to
hold certain elements of truth. And, if the armor and
the gold coins were real, then it seemed likely to the
Gunsmith that there really must be a hidden Spanish
treasure. He knew that the early conquistadors had
searched this country in the quest for the seven lost
cities of gold and some gold had been found.

Clint turned his face to the west where the golden sunset lit up the sky. He closed his eyes for a moment and envisioned a mountain of Spanish gold. Crazy, yes, but . . .

He did not see Deke whirl his horse around on the trail and race back up toward the pines, but one of the horses started in fear and its lead rope jerked the Gunsmith out of his fantasy and into the reality of the present.

"Hey!" he shouted. "Dammit, Deke, stop!"

But Deke had no intention of stopping. Even with his hands lashed behind his back, he was still able to ride like a wild man. It took Clint almost a full minute to ease Duke around the other horses and race after his escaped prisoner.

Duke was fast, strong, enabling Clint to overtake Deke in short order. But the trail was so narrow that Clint had trouble driving his horse in between Deke's struggling mount and the mountainside.

"Stop, you fool!" Clint shouted, leaning forward in his saddle and reaching for Deke's reins.

The bearded man was crazy to escape. He slammed his head forward like a battering ram against the Gunsmith's skull. If it had not been for his black Stetson, the blow would have split Clint's skull open like a gourd. As it was, it almost knocked him from his saddle and he was momentarily stunned.

Deke cursed wildly and tried to batter the Gunsmith again, but Clint managed to rear back in his saddle and Deke lost his balance. He leaned far out, unable to grab his saddle horn and right himself. With a shriek of terror, Deke lost his balance and fell. He struck Duke's hip and then was knocked back over the side of the mountain. Clint heard the man's scream vanish into the deep canyon below.

"Dammit!" he raged, pulling both horses to a standstill. He dismounted and ran back to the place where Deke had disappeared over the cliff. "Deke!"

There was no answer. Far below, in the fading light, Clint could see a sliver of water rushing through the bottom of the canyon. But no Deke.

"Deke! Can you hear me?"

Clint stared downward as dark shadows filled the abyss.

"Well, Deke, I guess you must have decided better this than a noose," Clint said into the fading light before he reined Duke around and headed on to Silver City.

It was well past midnight when the Gunsmith wearily pulled his horse up before the sheriff's office. The office was dark, but Clint knew that the sheriff might well be sleeping inside. Towns this size and smaller paid their lawmen such pathetic wages that many were forced to live in their cramped offices.

"Sheriff!" the Gunsmith called, pounding on the man's front door. "Sheriff, open up."

"Come back in the morning!" an angry voice replied.

"This won't wait! I got two dead men for you."

A long pause. "Take 'em to the mortician up the street and come back tomorrow."

Clint ground his teeth. What the hell kind of a sheriff was this, anyway? Clint walked back to the horses and led them up the street until he came to the funeral parlor, which also happened to be a barbershop. The sign on the door said that the proprietor was W. C. Apple.

Clint pounded on the front door. He kept pounding until he heard a shout from inside, and then a sleepy voice yelled, "Come back in the morning."

"I got two dead men."

A moment later, Clint heard Apple unlock his door. "Who are they?" the man asked, rubbing his eyes and standing in his nightshirt.

"One is named Henry. That's all I know. But the other is Abe Morton. Maybe you know him."

The mortician was a tall, stooped man in his fifties with a shock of gray hair and large bags under his eyes. "Yeah, I know Abe," he said, squinting out at the bodies draped over their horses. "He's got a daughter that lives here. Mrs. Annie Bates is a lovely woman. But unfortunately, she's married to a drunk and a womanizer. No one in this town can figure out why Annie doesn't throw him out the door. It's quite obvious that she's a very unhappy woman."

"That's a shame."

"Yeah," the mortician said, looking past Clint. "What happened to those two?"

"It's a long story," Clint said, "and I've had a long day. If you want. I'll help you carry in the bodies."

"Who's going to pay for their funerals?"

"Damned if I know."

"They have anything on 'em of value?"

"Yeah," Clint said. "They had horses and outfits. But we can go over all this in the morning."

The mortician yawned, stretched, and said, "All right, just so it's understood I don't do work for nothing. I'm a professional and professionals get paid."

"Sure," Clint said, a little irritably. "Give me a hand and let's get this done with."

In no time at all, they untied the bodies and carried them inside.

"We'll just lay them here on the floor next to my barber chair," Apple said. "I'll get 'em out before I open my barbershop in the morning."

"I'd think that would be a real good idea," Clint replied, trying to keep the sarcasm out of his voice. "By the way, where does Mrs. Annie Bates live?"

"Aw," the mortician said, "you don't have to worry about telling her about her father. Either I'll get around to doing it, or she'll heard the news on the street. Either way, she'll be around in the morning."

"I'd still like to see her," Clint said. "She might want to know exactly how her father died."

The mortician looked down at the dead old prospector. "He was beaten half to death, then shot in the chest. This other fella the one that did it?"

"That's right."

"Well, then," the mortician said, "I don't see what else there is to say about it. He got shot and you killed Abe's killer. Pretty simple, isn't it?"

Clint sighed. He was dog-tired and unimpressed with both Silver City's sheriff and its barber-sometimes-mortician. "If you need me, I'll be around."

"Where are their horses and outfits going to be?" Apple demanded. "I'll want to sell them tomorrow morning in order to cover my expenses."

"They'll be around too," Clint said, not liking the man's raw greed. "How much will it cost to plant them?"

"Abe's daughter will want a good service and casket. I'd guess his funeral will cost sixty dollars. This other fella, well, he'll get a ten-dollar pine box and the Lord's

Prayer spoken over his grave. Be twenty-five."

"I'll see that you're paid out of the proceeds of their horses, but I'm going to make sure that the prospector's daughter gets whatever money is left over."

W. C. Apple was insulted. "I'm an admirer of Mrs. Bates," he said stiffly. "I'd never take advantage of her in this time of grief, even though I disliked Abe."

"Fine," Clint said as he walked out the door, mounted Duke, and led the other three horses up the dark street toward a livery he had seen on an earlier visit.

It took him less than fifteen minutes to rouse the liveryman and arrange for the horses' care. It didn't take much longer than that to find a room at the Butler Hotel. Clint had stayed at the Butler Hotel on several occasions over the years, and he was immediately recognized by the sleepy-eyed old desk clerk.

"Mr. Adams! What a pleasure to see you."

"Thanks, George. I need a room and a bath."

"Cost you a little extra for the bath at this hour. I have to heat the water myself and haul it to your room."

"Here," Clint said, giving the old desk clerk an extra dollar. "I hope this is worth your trouble."

"It sure is!" George grinned. "You can have room number one hundred."

Clint accepted the key and found his own room. An hour later, freshly bathed, he slipped into bed and fell asleep, seduced by the dream of Spanish gold.

FOUR

The next morning Clint enjoyed a fine big breakfast and the attentions of a pretty young waitress who kept pouring him coffee.

"You're the man that everyone in Silver City is talking about," the waitress said in a low, husky voice. "You brought in Abe and another dead man last night."

"I did," Clint admitted.

He studied the handsome young woman. She was in her early twenties and had the broad, comely looks of a hearty Scandinavian. Her hair was blond, her shoulders and arms well-muscled, and she was a little wider across the beam than the Gunsmith liked. Despite that, there was a bold freshness in her eyes that Clint found very appealing.

"What's your name?"

"Sally," she said, looking pleased at his interest.

"Well, Sally, mine is Clint. You aren't wearing a ring. Are you married?"

"No."

"Engaged?"

She laughed. "No, are you?"

"Nope. When do you get off work?"

"My father owns this café. When business gets slow, I come and go as I want."

"I'm staying in room one hundred at the Butler Hotel. I've some people to see this morning. However, I'll make it a point to be free this afternoon."

The girl blushed. "What are you suggesting?"

Clint looked around. Some of the other customers were watching, but there was so much racket coming from the nearby kitchen that it was difficult to eavesdrop. "I'm suggesting that you might want to get better acquainted."

Her pale blue eyes widened. "Well," she whispered, "I don't know what kind of a girl you take me for."

"I don't take you for anything," Clint said. "I just thought you might want to come by for a visit this afternoon, that's all."

Sally left to serve other customers. She was trying very hard to look offended, but it wasn't working, and the Gunsmith caught her looking over at him a number of times. Clint paid his bill, left Sally a generous tip, and then headed off to visit Sheriff Edward Rudd.

"Hello," Clint said as he walked into the man's cluttered office. Sheriff Rudd was about what Clint had expected, given the man's earlier lack of professionalism. Rudd was short, pudgy, and his clothes were dirty and rumpled. He looked scruffy and inept. The Gunsmith wondered how the man had ever managed to get himself elected.

"My name is Clint Adams," the Gunsmith said as an introduction.

"Ah yes," the portly sheriff said, not bothering to remove his feet from his desk or even extend his hand. "You're the fella that brought the two bodies in last night."

"That's right."

"I already been over to see them at the mortician's parlor," the sheriff said. "I knew and liked Abe Morton, even if he was an ornery old bastard."

"What about the other man?"

"Never saw him before. What was his name?"

"Henry. He's the one that killed Abe. His partner was named Deke. The man threw himself off the side of a mountain last night. I can draw you a map to show where he went over, but it's going to be a hell of a job getting to the body. It's lost way down in the canyon."

"Then never mind that," the sheriff said. "I'm paid to protect the citizens of this town, not go galavantin' off after the bodies of strangers."

"Sure," Clint said, not surprised that the lazy-looking man showed no interest in going to investigate. "Has Mrs. Bates been told about the death of her father?"

"I imagine so," the sheriff said absently. "If she hasn't, she's the only one left in Silver City who isn't aware of Abe's death."

The sheriff frowned, then scratched his belly which strained hard against his soiled shirt. "Did Abe mention anything about Spanish gold?"

"As a matter of fact, he did. I'm sure that's why he was killed."

"Figures," the sheriff said matter-of-factly. "Everyone in town has heard that old geezer talk about buried treasure and lost mines for so many years that we all took him with a grain of salt. But then he goes runnin' off to Santa Fe, telling everyone about this Spanish fortune. I knew he was just asking for trouble."

"You almost sound like you think Abe Morton deserved to die," Clint growled.

"Oh, I didn't say that," the sheriff said quickly. "But Abe had a big mouth, especially when he was drinking."

"What about the Spanish gold coins he spent in Santa Fe? How did he get ahold of them?"

"I don't know," the sheriff admitted.

"Were there a lot of coins?"

"I'd guess a hundred. Enough to keep Abe drunk more often than sober."

"When did he first find them?"

"About three years ago. Caused quite a stir here in Silver City. Up until then, everyone thought he was just a loon. But after that, they started taking Abe seriously. A lot of would-be friends began to buy him drinks. But Abe wouldn't show them where he'd found those coins, and after a year or so, the interest died."

"What's your opinion?"

The sheriff frowned. "Those gold coins are certainly real, but Abe was such a fool that people really took advantage of him. What he didn't give away, he spent on drinks and gambling. He thought that he was a good poker player, but he wasn't. There were nights when he lost small fortunes. I think he ran out of the coins and there are no more to be found."

"I see," Clint said, not sure that he would have arrived at the same pessimistic conclusion. "Sheriff, last night I made it very clear to your mortician, Mr. Apple, that I wanted Abe's belongings and the proceeds from his horse and outfit to benefit his daughter."

"I'll handle that," the sheriff said, all at once quite the local official. "You're a stranger in this town, and I guess you'll probably be moving on today or tomorrow."

"I haven't decided yet," Clint said, sensing that the sheriff would have preferred that he leave Silver City. "Why do you ask?"

"No reason and no hurry," the sheriff assured him. "Tell me, what is your profession?"

"I'm a gunsmith."

"Your hands aren't those of a workingman."

Clint's brow furrowed. "What the hell is that supposed to mean?"

"I mean that you don't look like the kind of a man who earns his daily bread by the sweat of his brow. I'd take you for a gambler or . . . or maybe a gunfighter."

"I've been a lawman," Clint admitted. "But I'm a little too restless to settle in one place. So I set up shop in a town, enjoy my stay, and then move on when the itch to travel takes ahold."

"Must be a nice life," Rudd said. "If you've been a lawman, you know what a miserable existence it can be. The pay is awful and the risks are high."

"This seems like a pretty tame town you have."

"That's because I keep it that way, Mr. Adams. I allow no riffraff to stay in Silver City, and anyone without visible means of support will quickly arouse my suspicions."

"I see," Clint said, realizing that Rudd was giving him a warning. "If I decide to remain in Silver City, I'll try and remember to set up shop hours. Do you know of any gunsmithing work that needs doing?"

"Nope. We already have a man that repairs weapons. He's good, and he doesn't need any competition."

"Competition is the American way," Clint said. "Seems to me that corruption and laziness are to be found mostly in our public officials, many of whom take their jobs for granted after they're either appointed or elected."

It was Rudd's turn to blink. "Where are you staying?" he asked stiffly.

"Over at the Butler Hotel."

"Good. As for the horses and outfits that you brought those dead men in on last night, I'll handle their sale and the dispersion of the proceeds to the proper parties."

Clint started to object, but then he closed his mouth. He knew that Rudd was within his boundaries to take charge of this matter. The only problem was that Clint had an instinctive distrust of the lawman. He couldn't exactly say why, except that any man who kept himself and his office as dirty and disorganized as Sheriff Rudd was not someone who lived up to high personal standards. It was Clint's opinion that pride kept people honest, and when it was completely lacking—as in Sheriff Edward Rudd's case—dishonesty became the natural by-product or manifestation.

"Oh, and one other thing, Mr. Adams."

Clint had already started to leave the sheriff's office. Now he turned and looked back. "Yeah?"

"I'd like to know when you decide to leave town."

"Why?"

"Just a matter of information."

Clint walked outside, took a deep breath, and headed over to the livery to check on the horses.

That afternoon, he returned to his hotel and stretched out on the bed, thinking about taking a nap. Before he could drift off, however, there was a knock at his door.

Clint sat up. "Who is it?"

"Sally. Open up."

Clint grinned and went to the door. Sally was standing there looking sheepish. "I had to pay that nosy old desk clerk two bits to keep his mouth shut about this visit."

"Here," Clint said, reaching into his pockets and extracting two bits.

But Sally shook her head and pushed inside. She turned around and said, "That's not what I want in repayment."

Clint knew the look of a man-hungry woman. "No," he said, "I guess it isn't."

In a moment, they were in each other's arms, kissing. Sally's mouth opened, and Clint filled it with his tongue while his hands began to undress the young woman.

"Hurry," she whispered, fumbling with his belt.

It didn't take more than a few heart-pounding moments until Clint was on top of the woman, driving his stiff rod up into her strong and eager young body.

"Oh yes!" she whispered, her muscular legs reaching up and locking around his waist, her large breasts glistening with perspiration.

Clint growled low in his throat. He hadn't had a woman in several weeks, and he knew that he was carrying a full load. Slowly, working the girl to a fever pitch, he rode her until she was sweating, grunting, and gasping. When Sally's fingernails dug into his buttocks and her big bottom began to quiver, Clint unloaded his seed in thick torrents.

"That was wonderful," she panted.

"I'm glad that you approved," he said, thinking that this girl was pretty good in bed. "And guess what?"

"What?"

"There's a lot more to come."

She tightened on his manhood like a fist. "There had sure better be. Having you once would be like having just one piece of chocolate candy."

The Gunsmith chuckled. He'd received many compliments from women, but never one quite like that.

They made love all afternoon and when they were both exhausted, they dozed. Clint might have slept right on through the night except for a loud knocking at his door.

"Who is it?" he called, grabbing his pants.

"It's Mrs. Annie Bates. I . . . I need to talk to you about my father."

"Damn," Clint hissed as Sally pulled the bed sheet up to her neck. "Can you come back later?" he called out.

"No. Please. This is very important."

"Sally, would you crawl under the bed and hide?"

"What for?" she demanded with outrage. "Are you ashamed to be seen in bed with me?"

"Ah, hell. Never mind." Clint pulled on his shirt. He went and unlocked the door, then opened it a crack. "I was napping," he explained to a tall, dark-haired young woman. "Go on back down to the lobby, and as soon as I get fully dressed, I'll come down to meet you."

"Promise?"

"I promise."

"Thank you," Annie Bates said. "But please hurry. My husband doesn't know that I'm here. He wouldn't approve."

"I'll hurry," Clint promised, hearing the pleading in the woman's voice.

"Thank you."

When he closed the door, Sally jumped out of bed. "What the hell did you agree to meet her for?"

"Because I was with her father when he died."

"So?"

"So she's naturally going to want to know about his last few moments on earth."

"Just make sure that's *all* that Annie Bates wants," Sally warned.

"You've got a suspicious mind," Clint said. "Go back to bed. I'll be back in a few minutes."

Sally came waltzing over to him, broad hips swinging provocatively. "You'd better come back," she threatened. "Or I'll walk down those stairs just as I am and drag you back up here."

Clint gulped; he knew Sally wasn't bluffing.

FIVE

When the Gunsmith entered the lobby, he could see that Annie Bates was clearly distraught over the loss of her father. "I want to begin by saying how sorry I am about what happened to your father."

"Did you know him?"

Clint could see that George was hanging on their every word, so he said, "Why don't we go outside and take a walk?"

"I couldn't do that!"

"Why not?"

Annie glanced nervously at the door. "If my husband catches wind of this meeting, he will be terribly jealous. And if he found out that we went walking alone . . . well, it just wouldn't do. You see, he has a very bad temper, and I would never want to cause you trouble, Mr. Adams."

"How do you know my name?"

"The sheriff told me."

Annie moved out of George's hearing range and sat down on a rumpled sofa that was used by the hotel's guests. "Please, tell me what happened. Mr. Apple said that it would be better if this were a closed-casket funeral."

Clint understood. Apple was trying to shield Annie from seeing how bad her father had been beaten before he'd been murdered.

"The men that killed your father," Clint said, "were after the Spanish gold."

"Damn that gold!" she cried, jumping to her feet in anger. "Father would still be alive if he'd never found those accursed Spanish coins."

"I'm sure you're right," Clint said. "But you must understand that he died because he would not tell his captors where the gold was to be found. I can only think of one reason for his silence."

"What is that?"

"He wanted you to share in his fortune."

"Me?" Annie shook her head violently. "I told my father three years ago when he found those coins that they would only bring him suffering and pain. I also told him I wanted no part of that gold."

"He didn't believe you," Clint said. "With his dying breath, he whispered your name."

Fresh tears spilled down Annie's pale cheeks and a sob escaped her lips. "He did?"

"Yes."

"I don't know why."

"Are you already wealthy?" Clint asked.

She sniffled. "Of course not! Quite the opposite. Why do you ask such a question?"

"Because every father wants his children to be comfortable, to have nice things and not to have to worry about finances their whole lives long. I think that your father was no different. He had only one thing to give and that was the location of his Spanish treasure."

"Well, I don't want the damned thing!" Annie cried, starting to come to her feet and rush away.

Clint threw out his hand. "Listen," he said, "I don't know what happened before your father died or why you are so set against the Spanish gold. I do know this—your life might be in danger."

"What do you mean?"

"I mean that your father was drinking in Santa Fe, and he might have attracted other men like Deke and Henry. And when they discover that your father is dead, they'll just assume that you were in on his secret."

Annie stared. "You mean they'd think I knew where the gold was to be found?"

"Of course! If not you, then who else?"

Annie blinked. It was clear from her expression that she had never considered that her own life could be at risk. "Well, what am I to do?"

"I don't know," Clint said. "I think you should talk to Sheriff Rudd and explain the danger to him."

"He's worthless!"

"I'll speak to him."

"That would be useless."

Clint frowned. "What about your husband?"

"What about him?"

"I know this is a big step, but perhaps you might both consider leaving Silver City and moving to a new location where you are not so well-known."

Annie Bates shook her head. "My husband owns a mine claim, and it is paying. Not as well as he'd like, but it keeps a roof over our heads and he believes that it will one day provide us with a fortune."

"I see."

"My husband would *never* abandon his mining claim. He's spent the last five years working to develop it so that we are finally beginning to see some return."

Clint shrugged. "If the sheriff is as worthless as he appears, and as you claim, and if your husband will not take you away for your own safety, then I don't see that there is anything that can be done."

Annie looked into the Gunsmith's eyes. "Was my name really the last word he uttered before dying?"

"Yes, the very last."

Annie sobbed, and Clint instinctively drew her to his chest. "I'm very sorry," he said.

"Goddamn you, get away from my wife!"

Annie stiffened and pulled away from the Gunsmith. "Otis, please don't misunderstand. I was . . ."

"Yeah, I know." Otis snarled. "You were crying over that worthless father of yours while that son of a bitch was feeling your body up good. How does he feel?"

Clint felt his insides harden. "I think you owe your wife an apology and then you owe one to me."

"You can go to hell!"

Clint started forward and so did Otis, both with clenched fists.

"Please!" Annie cried. "Haven't I enough to worry about without you two fighting?"

Clint shook himself and lowered his fists, realizing that the young woman was extremely upset. And why wouldn't she be? She'd lost her father and was married to this jealous, raving maniac. It was a wonder that the poor woman even had a shred of sanity left.

"I'm sorry," he said to Annie. "You've been through a lot and whipping your husband isn't going to make things easier."

"Whipping me? Ha!"

Before Clint could react, Otis Bates was batting his wife aside and attacking the Gunsmith with both fists. Clint took two hard punches to the face and went down. Otis tried to stomp him with his boots, but his wife was screaming and pulling him aside so that the man was unable to do serious damage.

"Get him!" the old desk clerk shouted. "Clint, beat his gawddamn head in!"

When Otis lashed out with his boot, Clint managed to get his hands on the man's pant leg and drag him to the floor. Annie was wailing, but Clint didn't have time to worry about her because Otis was strong and crazy with anger. They were well-matched physically as they rolled about on the floor, Clint trying to protect his eyes from being gouged out while he pounded Otis in the face until it was bloody.

Finally, Otis's adrenaline began to stop pumping, and he began to slow down. Clint was able to jump up, set his feet, and then pound Otis with both fists as the man attempted to rise. A left hook ripped Otis's eyebrow open and a torrent of blood cascaded down his face. A wicked right uppercut caught Otis on the side of his jaw and flipped him over like a steak in a skillet.

"Stop it!" Annie screamed. "Please stop it!"

Otis was finished. He tried to get up but could only get to his knees. Clint lowered his hands and wiped his mouth with the back of his sleeve. "Mrs. Bates, I'm real sorry that this had to get so ugly."

"You ought to be sorry!"

"Why? We're the ones that were insulted. Can you tell me why your husband acts so crazy?"

Annie didn't have an answer, or at least not one that she could give to the Gunsmith. She knelt down beside her husband and tried to help him, but Otis doubled up his fist and took a swing at his wife. He caught her a glancing blow.

"Damn you!" Clint roared, pulling Annie away and stepping forward to drive a sweeping right which exploded against Otis's nose, cracking it like a walnut under a boot heel.

Otis bellowed with pain and crumpled forward.

The Gunsmith felt neither remorse, nor pity. The man had obviously been drinking, and he was dangerous. Furthermore, he treated his pretty wife worse than most men would treat their dog.

"Annie," he said, heading for his room, "that man is going to kill you, if someone doesn't kill him first. Get rid of him while you can."

But Annie just stared at him as he walked away.

Sally was waiting upstairs in the hall, and when she saw the blood on Clint's hands, she hurried to clean them with a washcloth.

"I opened the door, and I could hear Otis Bates shouting and cursing. I knew he'd go for you."

"He's a madman."

"He's scary," Sally said, patting Clint's scraped knuckles dry. "Now come to bed and let's forget all about them. Let's forget about everything except each other."

"I got no problem with that," Clint said, as Sally reached for his belt. "No problem at all."

SIX

The funeral for Abe Morton was nicer than Clint had expected. Annie looked splendid in the black crepe dress she wore for mourning. Hovering next to her and glaring with hatred was Annie's husband, and it was easy to see that he was wishing the Gunsmith was being buried too.

It was a raw, windy day, and very few other people attended besides the mortician and a few curious drunks that had often been the beneficiaries of Abe's generosity. The eulogy was brief, but eloquent, and the Gunsmith, who considered himself somewhat of an expert on funerals, was impressed.

"Nice work, Mr. Apple," Clint said when the funeral service ended.

"Well thank you," the man replied rather solemnly. "I take all these occasions quite seriously."

"So I see."

Apple leaned forward and whispered, "If you don't watch your back, Mr. Adams, Otis Bates will have me arranging *your* funeral."

"I know what you mean," Clint said, "and I appreciate your warning."

Clint stepped back and replaced his hat on his head. And then, since it was considered good manners to extend one's condolences to the bereaved, he went over to Annie, wondering if her jealous husband with his swollen and discolored broken nose would be foolish enough to go for his gun.

"Mrs. Bates, please accept my sincere regrets. I didn't know your father except for the very last moments of his life, but even that was enough to make me realize that the man was good and brave."

"Thank you for coming," Annie said nervously. "You could have just left his body out there in the wilderness. I'm sure that would have been much less trying, but you didn't. I'll always be grateful to you for allowing me to bury him."

"I'm honored that I was able to extend that small service," Clint said gallantly, knowing that Otis Bates was very near the point of going for his gun.

"Get away from my wife!" Bates hissed.

Clint smiled. "If you went for your gun, you'd be doing everyone and especially your wife a great favor because I'd kill you."

Bates's jaw dropped, and before the man could react, Clint turned on his boot heel and walked away.

That afternoon, Sheriff Rudd paid him a visit at the hotel. Clint invited the man inside his room and said, "Have a seat on the bed."

"No thanks," Rudd said, looking at the rumpled mass of covers. "I understand that you and Sally have taken up company."

The Gunsmith's eyebrows raised. "Is that anyone's business?"

"Could be," Rudd said. "Sally is wild and not of the highest moral fiber, but her father is a friend of mine and I like the girl. I just don't want to see her hurt by a drifter."

"Oh." Clint's voice took on an edge. "So are you representing the law in Silver City, or the clergy?"

"I'm just saying that Sally is basically a good girl, and I expect you to behave yourself. Let me be blunt. Don't leave her with a child."

Clint was getting angry. "Sheriff Rudd, if that's all you came to talk about, I think it would be best if you just got the hell out of here."

"Now wait a minute! I came to talk to you about something else."

"What?" Clint demanded.

"About that Spanish gold." The sheriff sighed. "There's been a few strangers drifting into my town, and I was wondering if maybe they're on the trail of that hidden fortune."

Clint shrugged, thinking that they probably were. "That's possible. Are you worried about me?"

"Hell no!"

"Then why the warning?"

The sheriff steepled his fingers and leaned forward. "Do you know where that treasure is hidden?"

The Gunsmith barked a laugh. "Hell no! If I knew where a fortune in Spanish gold was hidden, would I be sitting around here?"

"You've been doing more screwing than sitting, I'd wager," the sheriff said, "and a good-looking girl like Sally is enough to hold any man down for a while.

I always thought I'd like to sample a little of that sweet-meat pie myself."

Clint stifled an urge to walk over and smack the sheriff between the eyes. He decided to hear the man out because, quite obviously, something was working on his devious little mind.

"Get to the point of your visit," Clint ordered.

"Ah yes, the point." Rudd grinned. "I think you *do* know where that Spanish gold is buried. Or at least, you have a general idea."

The sheriff peered intently at the Gunsmith, hoping for some telltale response but getting nothing. "Very well then," he continued, "I can understand why you'd be closemouthed. But the truth of the matter is that you need a partner."

"For what?"

"To find that gold! And then, to bring it out safely. One man can't work and keep his back covered at the same time."

"And so you're offering to be my partner?"

"That's right."

"What about your job?"

"I'll quit. I could work here for twenty more years and not make enough money to buy even a poor spread."

Rudd leaned back. "What do you say? You need a partner that knows this country inside and out. I'm thinking you probably don't know exactly where the treasure is buried. Maybe you just have a piece of the map. Maybe Mrs. Bates has a piece. We put them together and . . ."

"Annie doesn't have a piece of anything, and you'd better leave her the hell out of this."

"Sure," Rudd said, his greedy smile dying. "I just threw that out as a possibility. I thought maybe you and her had shared a little information and that's when her husband found you together and you had to whip his ass."

"All she wanted to know was how her father spent his last few moments," Clint said. "And I was able to tell her that Abe Morton died thinking of her."

"Shee-it! That old man thought of nothing except whiskey and gold. I know it, you know it, and even Annie knows it."

"Sheriff Rudd, I think," Clint said, advancing on the lawman, "that this unpleasant little visit of yours has about run its course."

"Now wait a minute! You can take sixty percent of the gold. I'll settle for less than half."

"I'll just bet you would," Clint said with disgust. "You'd walk out on Silver City and never look back."

"I don't owe these people a damn thing. They pay me almost nothing and expect me to lay my life down for them whenever there's trouble."

Clint stepped forward and his hand shot out to grab Rudd's badge.

"Hey!" the man cried, trying to pull away. "What are you . . . ?"

The Gunsmith tore the badge from Rudd's shirt and hurled it through the open window.

"What the hell did you do that for?"

"It looks better on dirt than on you," Clint snarled. "Now get the hell out of this room before I throw *you* out the window."

Rudd backed up fast, but he was wagging his finger

every step of the way. "You think that you're such a big deal, don't you? You think that you're going to find that gold and get it to some bank all by yourself. Well, you're dead wrong!"

"Am I?"

"That's right. There are men in this town looking for you at this very moment. They won't pussyfoot around you like I've been doing. They'll come and you'll either tell them what you know, or they'll blow holes in your head. Do you understand me?"

"Sure. You're saying that unless I cooperate with you, I'd damn sure better not count on the law. Isn't that right?"

"Exactly."

The Gunsmith was so angry that he rushed the man, grabbed him by his shirtfront, and propelled him out of his room, slamming him up against the opposite wall. Rudd's eyes bulged with fear when Clint doubled up his fist and cocked it back.

"If you hit me, you'll be charged with assaulting an officer of the law!" the man screeched.

"You're a disgrace!" the Gunsmith raged, slamming the door shut behind him.

It took several hours and a couple of drinks before Clint calmed down enough to leave the hotel. He did not know the people of Silver City by their faces, so he'd have to find someone that he could trust to point out the strangers intent on finding him and making him tell them where the Spanish gold was buried.

"Did Abe really know himself?" Clint asked aloud as he walked down the street, senses tingling with the feel of danger in the air.

Clint knew that the answer would come sooner rather than later. He also knew that if there really was a buried Spanish treasure, the only person on this planet who could help him find it was Annie Bates.

SEVEN

Clint went over to the stable to check on Duke and the other horses that he'd brought down from the mountains. His big, black gelding stood several inches taller than the rest of the horses in the corral.

"He can be an ornery bastard with other stock, can't he?" the liveryman said when he came over to join the Gunsmith. "I've had to take him out and feed him by hisself. Otherwise, he just runs them other horses off until he's had his fill."

Clint nodded. "He's learned to fight for his food, all right. Are you going to offer me a price for these horses, or shall I run them and their saddles over to Santa Fe or maybe even El Paso where I know that I can get top dollar?"

"You'd do that?"

"I would."

"Mr. Apple wouldn't be too damned pleased and neither would the sheriff. And for that matter, Otis Bates has already been over here askin' about this stock. He figures that their sale money ought to go to his wife."

"She'd never see a penny of it," Clint said.

"You got that right. But Otis, he's got a real hatred for you on account of the way you broke his nose and battered the hell out of his face."

"Some things are just not worth worrying about," Clint said. "And Otis Bates isn't the kind I'd lose a lot of sleep over. He's a hotheaded fool."

"He's not afraid of a fight."

"I know that," Clint said, "but he's not half as tough as he thinks. Can he shoot a gun?"

"Damn right he can! One of the best men with a side arm in this part of New Mexico. He's spent a lot of time practicin' his fast draw too."

The liveryman let his eyes drop to the gun on Clint's hip. "You're also pretty damn good with a six-shooter, from what I hear."

"I can use one," Clint said laconically. "Now, give me your best offer for these horses."

"Thirty-five dollars."

"Forty, and that's dirt-cheap considering the saddles and gear that you'll get with each animal. I expect that you'll make at least twenty-five dollars on every outfit."

"Twenty, maybe."

"Well," the Gunsmith said, "forty, or I'm leaving in the morning."

"What about the feed I already put into 'em?"

"They appreciate that, and so do I. The price is still forty dollars."

"You're a tough bastard to deal with, Adams. Real tough. I have a hunch that you're bluffing."

"What makes you think that?"

"Sally is a real frisky gal."

"She'll still be here when I come back. The price is forty dollars. Take it or leave it."

"I'll take it," the liveryman snorted.

"Good. Where's the cash?"

"In my bank."

"Then let's get over there and close the deal."

The liveryman scratched himself, then reluctantly nodded. "You are a hard, hard man to do business with."

Clint just smiled. Some men would dicker forever and enjoy every minute of it, but the Gunsmith was not one of them. He would counter an offer a few times, then take his stand. Most often, he'd arrive at a satisfactory price or else he'd walk away without any regrets.

The liveryman introduced himself as Jim Beech on the way to the bank. Getting him to withdraw his money was a slow process, but Clint was patient. Abe Morton's horse money, of course, would go to his daughter, and Clint would sweeten the deal with half the proceeds from the other two horses as well.

"Well," Beech grumped, "there you are, one hundred and twenty dollars."

"Which I'll split down the middle with Mrs. Bates," Clint said.

"She can use the money," Beech replied. "Her husband spends it like water. If he isn't drinkin' money up, he's spending it on bullets and . . ."

"Where have you been?" Sally called, hurrying over to join them. "Clint, I've been looking all over the place for you."

"I had to sell a couple of horses," Clint said with an amused grin. "Mr. Beech skinned me pretty good."

"The hell I did! I paid top dollar for them horses he brought in, Sally."

Sally looked from one man to the other, then said, "Well, Jim, everybody in Silver City knows that you're worth more than anyone else in these parts. They say that you could buy half the town, if you weren't so tightfisted."

"Ha!"

Clint chuckled. It was clear that Sally and Jim were well acquainted and enjoyed teasing each other. Clint listened for a few moments, then he took Sally's arm. "How about we go and have ourselves a good dinner on me tonight?"

"Now *that* would be a change."

Clint took the girl's arm and started to turn, but just then Jim Beech shouted, "Look out!"

The Gunsmith's hand flashed toward his six-gun, but his thumb accidentally hooked in Sally's dress. The delay took only a split second, less than the time it took for a man to blink, but it was enough time for Otis Bates to unleash three bullets.

Clint heard the first one strike Sally. She groaned and dropped. The second bullet was wild, and the third hit Jim Beech, knocking the man sideways to the ground.

"You crazy bastard!" Clint shouted, his own gun bucking in his fist so rapidly that his shots were like rolling thunder.

Bates began to stagger backward. His gun coughed bullets into the street, then as he began to topple, into the sky. He was still firing when he hit the ground.

"Sally!" Clint shouted, knowing that the girl had been badly wounded. "Sally!"

She was dead, shot through the heart. Tears filled

Clint's eyes, and he had to force himself to go over to Jim Beech. "Jim, how bad are you hit?"

"It's bad," the liveryman wheezed.

Clint saw the stain of dark blood spreading across Jim's shirtfront. He tore the shirt open and stared at the wound.

"Am I lung-shot?" Beech whispered.

"No," Clint said, noting that the wound was too high and wide to strike the lung. Most likely, it had struck the collarbone and splintered it, then maybe even gone through the man.

"We need a doctor!" Clint shouted. "Someone find a doctor!"

People who had just started to come out of their buildings dashed back into them, and Clint hoped that one of those people was going to get a doctor. "Just hang on, Jim."

"Doc Murphy is a good man," Beech wheezed, his face pale, his voice dry and weak. "If I ain't lung-shot, he might be able to save me."

"Sure he will." Clint tore a handkerchief from his back pocket and pressed it to the wound to stop the hemorrhaging. "You just take it easy and you'll be just fine."

In a few minutes that seemed like a few hours, a thirtyish-looking doctor came dashing over to them. He grabbed Clint's wrist and pulled the handkerchief aside, then studied the bullet wound.

"Jim, you're going to live," he said in a calm, assured voice. "You might not have the full use of your left shoulder, but you're going to pull through this if you don't panic."

"I ain't going to panic, but it hurts. How is Sally? I

want you to take care of her, Doc."

"She's dead," Clint said. "Sally took a bullet through the heart. She was probably dead before she hit the street."

Tears filled Jim's eyes. "Son of a bitch! Goddamn that Bates! Adams, you better find and kill him or I will!"

"It's done," Clint said. "I dropped Bates. He won't be hurting anyone again."

Jim nodded his pointy, whiskered chin. "It's a bad trade, Sally for Bates. A bad trade."

"Let's get this man to my office," the doctor said, gently rolling the liveryman over on his side and examining his back for an exit wound.

"Ahh!"

"Easy," the doctor said. "Jim, the good news is that the bullet passed right through your shoulder. That means that I'm not going to have to dig it out. But I am afraid that your shoulder might be a little worse for the wear."

"To hell with it."

The Gunsmith signaled for a couple of the spectators to help him carry the wounded man to the doctor's office. Jim was crying and wailing in both anger and pain.

"Adams!"

Clint turned to see Sheriff Rudd. "What do you want?"

"I think we had better have another talk."

But Clint shook his head. "There's nothing for us to talk about, Sheriff. Nothing new."

"You don't think so? I could arrest you."

"For what? Defending myself and killing a murderer?"

Sheriff Rudd's lips pinched together. "You're big trouble. You attract killing like shit attracts flies."

Clint took a deep breath, and then he started for the sheriff. Reading his eyes, Rudd had the sense to backpedal. "Now don't you go crazy! I'm an officer of the law."

The Gunsmith's fingers dug into the sheriff's coat, and he shook the man until his teeth rattled. "Rudd, my patience has run out with you. Stay away from me or risk the consequences."

"You can't threaten an officer of the law!"

"No threat," Clint said. "A promise. Cross me again, and I will make you pay."

Clint might have said more except that Annie Bates came racing across the street to throw herself down beside the body of her husband.

"What happened?" she cried. "Who killed Otis?"

"I did," the Gunsmith said. "He tried to gun me down, only his aim was bad. He killed Sally by accident and wounded Jim Beech."

Annie had not even noticed Sally's body, probably because it was surrounded by a crowd of curious onlookers. But now, as the Gunsmith's words sank in and she saw the dead woman, she understood the tragic enormity of her husband's violent actions.

"Oh, no!" she cried, recoiling from her husband and running over to stand and stare at Sally's body and the massive bloodstain that covered her bosom. "No!"

Several women took Annie away. Clint heard her wailing in grief, and he just hoped that she was wailing over the innocent Sally and not her monster of a husband.

EIGHT

Otis Bates was buried in the morning without a sermon or anyone to attend his funeral except his wife Annie and W. C. Apple, the town mortician. The Gunsmith watched the pair ride the hearse out to the cemetery, and he was still looking out his hotel room window when the same hearse returned to Silver City in less than an hour.

Sally's afternoon funeral was both elaborate and well-attended. The gunsmith hadn't realized how popular she had been until he saw the huge crowd that came to pay their last respects. A hat had been passed around the saloons and a donation box had been available at her father's restaurant for anyone and everyone who wished to contribute to Sally's funeral. Clint heard that the people of Silver City had donated over two hundred dollars for the funeral.

W. C. Apple really outdid himself that cool, blustery afternoon, and when he finished his eulogy, there were very few dry eyes among those who had come to pay Sally their respects.

"She was a friend to everyone she met," Apple said in conclusion, "and the Lord will welcome her into his heavenly kingdom. Amen."

But after the funeral was over, Clint was shocked when Sally's father came over and cried, "Adams, I blame *you* for this! If my daughter hadn't met you, she would still be alive!"

The Gunsmith looked into the man's suffering, blood-shot eyes and spoke no easy words of denial. "You're right," he admitted. "The bullet that killed your daughter had my name on it, and I'm sorry."

"No you're not! You're *alive*! It's my daughter who has just been buried."

"I *am* sorry," Clint repeated. "Your daughter was a fine young lady. If I could do anything more than kill the man who shot her, I would."

Sally's father sobbed. He was a pale, weary-looking man in his late fifties and aging fast. His eyes glistened with tears, and he had difficulty speaking. "I always thought that Sally would come to no good end because of a man like you. She couldn't tell the good ones from the bad."

Clint stood stony-faced and took the grieving father's abuse. It was not the first time he'd done so, for he had been forced to kill in the past, and there was always someone grieving and ready to fix blame.

"Here," Clint said, taking his share of the horse sale money out of his pockets. "Maybe . . ."

"You think you can *buy* yourself out of what you did?"

"No."

"Then get away from me! Get out of Silver City! Since you've come here, there has been too damn much dying. Two buried only a few days ago, then two more today."

"I'm not responsible for the killing that other men do," Clint said before he turned away and started to walk back to Silver City.

"Where are you going?" Sheriff Rudd asked, slightly out of breath from his mild exertion as he caught up with the Gunsmith on the road back into town.

"It's time to leave," Clint said. "Sally's father was right about at least one thing, the only person that would hate to see me leave Silver City is your mortician, Mr. Apple."

"What about the Spanish gold?"

Clint stopped and faced the man. "Are you still thinking about that?"

Rudd shifted uneasily. "Who wouldn't think about all that gold? And that offer I made earlier about us becoming partners, well, it still stands."

"Yeah," Clint said drily, "I'll bet it does."

The sheriff flushed with anger. "Gawddammit! You need my help to find that gold and fight off the vultures that will trail you as if you were a dying dog!"

"No I don't," Clint said, walking away from the man. "I don't need or want your help."

Clint returned to his hotel room and quickly packed his saddlebags. Just being in the room where he and Sally had enjoyed so many hours of laughter and love-making was difficult. He could smell the scent of her and feel her presence everywhere he turned. It was definitely time to ride out. But before leaving, Clint made sure that he still had the half of the treasure map that he had taken from Deke.

"Probably just a wild-goose chase anyway," he muttered to himself.

"Checking out, huh?" the hotel clerk said when Clint walked past with his bags. "I guess that you're probably going to go treasure hunting now."

Clint halted at the door. "To be honest with you, I don't even know if there is any Spanish gold. But I do know that far too many people have already died over something that may not even exist."

"Really?" the desk clerk asked, looking surprised, then skeptical.

"That's right. I was enjoying myself trout fishing up in the mountains when this miserable Spanish treasure business happened. I didn't ask for Abe Morton or his killers to come barging into my camp. I got dragged into all this killing when all I wanted was a little peace and solitude."

"Peace and solitude?" a voice said from behind. "I don't think so. Men like you attract trouble."

Clint turned to see Annie Bates standing in the doorway. She wasn't smiling. "I haven't had the chance to tell you that I'm sorry that things worked out the way they did. You've lost a father and now a husband."

"I lost a father and a man who had changed so much I hardly knew him anymore. Even I have to remind myself that my late husband wasn't always consumed by greed, jealousy, and hatred."

Clint relaxed. "It happens to men, especially when they catch gold fever. Your husband was a miner, wasn't he?"

"Yes." Annie glanced at the desk clerk, who was listening intently. "I can see that you are leaving town. But first, I'd like to have a word with you in private."

"Sure," Clint said, and then could not resist adding, "but do you think it's such a good idea to be seen with a man who always attracts trouble?"

Annie blushed with embarrassment. "I'm sorry. I had no right to say that, especially considering how you brought my father down from the mountains."

The Gunsmith took Annie's arm and led her outside and down the boardwalk. When they neared the livery, he tried to give Annie all the horse sale money, but she refused to take any payment other than what her father's horse and outfit had been worth.

"I want to talk to you about the Spanish gold," she said when they were alone.

"It's cursed," the Gunsmith said, surprised by the passion in his own voice. "It's brought nothing but death."

"My father spoke of it many times. He *knew* where it was hidden, and I think maybe you do too."

"I don't." Clint removed the piece of the treasure map from his pocket, unfolded it, and handed it to Annie. "Before your father died, the men who killed him managed to get this map. It's incomplete, as you can see."

"Yes," Annie said, studying the map intently. "Did my father tell you anything about the missing half?"

"The only thing he was able to say before he died was your name. I took that to mean that you're the only one who might know where the second half of the map is now, or else he described to you where the treasure is hidden."

Annie looked away quickly. "May I keep this, or are you really going treasure hunting?"

"You can keep it," the Gunsmith said. "But I think it will bring you even more tragedy."

"Why?"

"Because the sheriff told me there are already men in Silver City determined to find that gold. They think I know where it's hidden, but I don't."

"Then it seems to me, Mr. Adams, that your life is very much in danger."

"Clint," he corrected, "and yes, I'll have to watch my back trail. But you need to understand that your father was tortured then shot for that little scrap of paper you are holding. It would not be altogether surprising if *your* life were also in jeopardy."

Rather than acting shocked, Annie nodded. "The thought has occurred to me."

"So what are your plans?"

"I think I may leave Silver City."

"That would be smart."

"To hunt for my father's buried treasure," she added.

"That would *not* be smart. In fact, it would be extremely unwise."

"Not if I had protection."

"It's your neck, but I don't advise going after that Spanish gold, if there even is such a thing."

"Oh, there is! In fact, I have some locked away at my house."

"Really?"

"Yes. I wouldn't even tell my husband what I've just confessed. He would have torn our home apart board by board and then dug up the foundation hunting for the gold coins my father left in my care."

"Why didn't you just put them in the bank?"

"If I had," Annie said, "everyone in town would have known about them, and that would have created a stampede into the mountains. My father warned me of that when he was sober. I agreed with him."

"Why are you telling me all this?"

"Because I want you to help me find the Spanish treasure that cost my father his life."

"Why me?"

"Why not? You've already demonstrated that you are a gunman and a survivor. I think you are the only man that really could help me find my father's treasure."

"How much do you know?"

Annie shrugged. "I know quite a lot. And coupling what I know along with this map—even though we're missing the part that actually details where the Spanish gold is hidden—should enable us to find the treasure."

"And what then?" Clint asked quietly.

"Then we take the Spanish gold to Santa Fe and put it in the bank."

"And what is my cut?"

"Half. No more, no less."

"That's generous."

"You'll earn your money. As you said, there are already men in town that are watching your every move. It will be up to you to somehow throw them off our trail and then help me find and extract the treasure."

"I see." Clint's mind was racing. "Did your father ever say exactly how much gold he'd uncovered?"

"Yes. About five hundred pieces are left buried up in those mountains. We wouldn't be rich, but we'd never have to worry about money again."

Clint agreed. The Spanish gold pieces were worth at least a hundred dollars each, possibly much more in the East. "Why have you decided to trust me?"

"Who said that I do?"

"But . . ."

"I have no choice but to trust you," Annie admitted. "There is no one else. I couldn't even trust my husband. Besides, I'm thinking that my father just might have told you more than you are willing to admit."

"That's not true, and you'd better understand that right now," Clint said.

"That changes nothing," Annie said. "I still want and need your help. I know that you turned down Sheriff Rudd, please don't do the same to me."

"You're much more appealing than the sheriff."

Annie stepped back, and her voice took on an edge and a warning. "Please do us both a favor and understand something, Mr. Adams. If we go treasure hunting together, that's *all* we do together. Is that clear?"

"Very."

"Good. Do we have a deal?"

Clint thought about it for a moment, then said, "Annie, do you swear on your father's grave that there really is gold to be found?"

"I do. Otherwise, what is the point?"

"There is no point without the gold." Clint sighed. "All right, we'll go find it together."

Annie smiled, something that Clint had not seen her do before. "Thank you, Clint."

"You're welcome. How soon can you leave?"

"I can leave tonight under the cover of darkness and meet you somewhere in the foothills. It wouldn't be wise to be seen riding out of Silver City together."

"I suppose not." Clint turned and looked up at the Mogollons. "Let's meet this side of where the trail gets steep on the mountainside."

"The place where that man Deke went over?"

"Yes."

"I'll see you there soon after midnight."

Annie turned to leave, but Clint grabbed her arm. "One thing," he said, "I won't appreciate it if you have some other purpose in mind."

"What do you mean?"

"I don't know, exactly. I just want it to be very clear between us that you really do have a good idea where the Spanish gold is to be found."

"All right. I can tell you this—it may take a few hard weeks of searching, but we'll find that treasure. I swear we will."

"That's all I wanted to know," the Gunsmith replied as he started for the livery.

NINE

It was well past midnight when the Gunsmith decided that something must have gone wrong. Annie should have been out to meet him, and he was worried that something was badly amiss.

Tightening his cinch, Clint remounted Duke and galloped back into town. He knew where Annie lived, and he dismounted and tied Duke several doors away. Drawing his gun, he circled Annie's small clapboard house and came up to the back door.

There was a faint lamplight burning inside, and the Gunsmith had a sixth sense that told him something really was amiss. Opening the back door, Clint stepped into the dim hallway which led into a kitchen. He stopped and listened for voices. He heard nothing, but the hairs on the back of his neck were standing up in warning as he began to tiptoe forward.

A flash of gunfire was instantly followed by the explosion of a six-gun. Clint instinctively threw himself sideways, and his own gun bucked twice. He saw a dark silhouette topple forward and strike the floor.

"Annie!"

The Gunsmith heard the sound of boots slamming out the front of the house. Clint stepped over the body of the man he'd just shot and started to run after the fleeing man, but Annie's muffled voice stopped him in the dim hallway.

"Annie, where are you?"

She grunted and banged on the wall. The Gunsmith stepped into a bedroom, and although it was very dim, he saw the young woman lying on her bed, bound and gagged. He hurried over and removed the gag.

"Are you all right?"

"No, I'm *not* all right!" she cried, sobbing brokenly. "Untie my wrists and ankles, and let's get out of here."

"I just shot a man. We can't leave him here."

"Then let's take him up the street and dump him!" Annie exclaimed. "Clint, the one that got away will bring others. We can either run for our lives, or forfeit our lives."

"I should get the sheriff," Clint said stubbornly. "He is the law in this town."

"He's probably one of them."

The Gunsmith realized that Annie might be correct. Sheriff Rudd was so greedy, he would do anything to find the Spanish treasure and become a wealthy man.

"All right," Clint said, untying Annie. "Are you ready to ride?"

"Sure! I was heading out the back door to mount my horse when they jumped me."

Clint lit a match and held it over the face of the dead man that he'd shot. "Do you recognize him?"

"No."

The Gunsmith grabbed the dead man and pulled him erect, then dropped him over his shoulder. "Let's go."

Clint didn't know if the gunshots had awakened the neighbors or not, but he really did not care. As quickly as possible, he retrieved Duke, and then they found Annie's horse. Clint loaded the dead man across his saddle and led Duke a block away. He dumped the body in an alley, then mounted his horse.

"I imagine someone might have seen us, and this won't throw the sheriff or anyone else off our tracks," he said. "I expect we better watch our back trail."

"We will," Annie vowed. "I'd bet anything that the sheriff and some of the others involved in this are already starting for my house."

"There may not be much left of it when you come back," Clint warned. "They'll probably turn it upside down looking for the treasure map or anything else that will give them a lead as to our destination."

"They'll find nothing," Annie said with no small amount of satisfaction in her voice. "I either sold or gave away everything of any value that I owned. If they burned the house down, it wouldn't be worth as much as a dozen of the golden Spanish coins that we're going to find."

"All right. Just as long as you know," Clint said.

"All I know is that we are going to become rich and that my father won't have died needlessly."

The Gunsmith gave Duke free rein, and the animal raced out of town with Annie quirting her mare hard to keep pace. They galloped for two miles. Finally, when they were on the narrow mountain trail, Annie cried, "Hold up!"

"What's wrong?" Clint asked, drawing in his big gelding to a walk.

"It's my mare," Annie said. "She's not used to being ridden, and she's out of condition. We've been running uphill since leaving Silver City. I'll kill her if she doesn't have a chance to catch her wind."

Clint only had to listen to the winded mare to realize the truth of Annie's words. The mare was a pretty sorrel with a blazed face and three white stockings. She was sleek, fat from being grained and curried to excess, and totally out of trail condition. She had a beautiful head, wide across the eyes but very tapered in the muzzle, and a long, flaxen mane and tail.

"Annie, that mare might be the death of us," Clint warned. "The men who will climb up our back trail will be riding tough horses like mine. We can't be held up until that mare is toughened up by miles of rugged mountain trails."

"She is an Arabian," Annie said. "I bought her from a traveling man down on his luck. He said that Arabians are the toughest horses alive."

"I don't believe that."

"I do," Annie said. "I've heard stories about them."

The Gunsmith was not in the least bit impressed. "Yeah? Well look at her. She's blowing like an old man that's been run up a tree."

"She'll need a day or two to catch her stride and get her wind back," Annie said defensively. "But after that, she'll keep that big, black gelding of yours huffing and puffing."

They waited in silence while the horses caught their breath. Clint could see that Annie wasn't about to part with the sorrel Arabian mare, and that there was no use in suggesting they trade her for a mustang or the first good mountain horse they happened to come across.

"All right," he said, "but if she goes lame, sours, or quits up in the Mogollons, you'll be walking."

"I'll take that risk," Annie snapped. "Now, are we going to sit here and talk until sunrise, or are we going to put some more miles between us and whoever might be getting ready to follow us up from Silver City?"

Clint returned his attention to the winded sorrel and was surprised to see that it was indeed already breathing easier and seemed to be recovering very fast. Maybe the drummer had known what he was talking about when he had praised the Arabians as a breed that possessed great heart and stamina.

"Let's go," he said, riding higher into the mountains.

For the rest of that night, the Gunsmith pushed hard and used a few of his tricks to confuse anyone trying to follow their tracks. He followed the mountain trail, but then he left it and rode over shale and up a small stream to throw off pursuit. By the time the sun crested the eastern peaks, they were high in the Mogollon Mountains and facing range after range of peaks as far as the eye could see.

"Annie, I think we had better stop worrying about someone following us and start thinking about that Spanish gold. Which direction should we start heading in?"

Annie dismounted and let her mare blow. The Arabian's head hung knee-high, and she was covered with sweat. Just four or five hours of hard mountain climbing had reduced her from a pretty town horse fit for a rich lady or a carriage to a worn-out animal that looked as if she were about to drop from weariness.

"We need to ride west," Annie said, pointing. "Over those mountains."

"Do we rejoin the Gila River?"

"Yes."

"Then maybe we ought to just . . ."

"Please," Annie said. "I've memorized every detail of my father's map. But in order to follow it to the treasure, we have to begin at the beginning."

"What does that mean?"

"It means that we must ride until we come to a certain odd-looking peak. That is the starting point."

"Can't we just skip it and move to a midpoint on the map and save ourselves some hard riding?"

"No," Annie said without hesitation. "I have to find every landmark and check them off one by one like a shopping list. Otherwise, I'll never find the treasure. Trust me, Clint. My father was very smart, and he had his own way of doing things. His map wasn't meant to be read logically. It has special and secret meanings that only I can read."

"I just hope this isn't a wild-goose chase."

"It isn't," Annie vowed. "I'm not out here with you half killing my pretty mare and looking over my shoulder every other minute in order to play games."

Clint supposed that this was true. "Here," he said, handing his reins to Annie. "I'm going to climb up on that rock and have a look down our trail and see if I've shaken the pursuit."

"You aren't sure?"

"No," Clint said. "A good tracker would read through all my little detours and ruses. I'm good, but not good enough to fool an expert Apache tracker."

Annie's brow knitted. "You don't really think that . . ."

"The men who are going to follow us believe that there is a Spanish fortune waiting to be unearthed somewhere in these mountains," Clint said. "Given that, I don't find it so unreasonable that the people who are trying to take it would hire an Apache."

"No," Annie said, looking worried, "I suppose not."

Clint reached out and touched her arm. "Don't be too upset. I have a tendency to make things sound worse than they are. We've done some hard riding, and it would be very difficult to pick up our tracks for the first few miles out of Silver City because that road is so well-traveled."

"I see."

"In order to distinguish our tracks from all the others, one of our horses would have to have something special."

"You mean be wearing a special shoe? Something like that?"

"Exactly."

"I hate to tell you this," Annie replied, "but my mare does have a special shoe on her right front foot."

"What?"

"It's a bar shoe. She had an old injury, and the bar protects her frog from rock damage."

Clint dismounted. Without a word, he went over to the Arabian mare and lifted her right forefoot and studied the shoe. "Damn!"

"Pretty important, huh?"

"You bet it is," Clint said. "I sure wish you'd told me about this bar shoe before we left. It will be easy for even a halfway decent tracker to pick out among hundreds of other hoofprints. It's as if we've been leaving a mark every foot of the way telling them exactly where we've been."

"I'm sorry. But what can we do?"

By way of a reply, the Gunsmith reached out and began to rip apart Annie's riding skirt.

"Hey! What are you doing?"

Clint tore a little more until he had about a two-foot square. "This will have to do until I can get some leather padding to cover the hoof," he said. "But before I put it on, we need to get back on the main road where there are lots of other tracks. That way they won't know what to think."

Five minutes later, the Gunsmith had the patch wrapped and tied around the mare's right front hoof and was covering his own boot prints before remounting.

"That ought to give whoever is following us something to think about," he said, satisfied with his handiwork.

"Do you think they will be fooled?"

"No, but it will make their job a whole lot more difficult," the Gunsmith replied.

"Will it stay?"

"It had better."

"Or what?" Annie asked.

"Or you're going to have to make a choice between my company or that of your mare."

"I think I like the company of my mare better," Annie said, clearly miffed.

"That's your choice," Clint said. "But if they catch up with you, that mare isn't going to put up half the fight that I will. Think about it."

Annie lapsed into a brooding silence as they continued higher into the Mogollon Mountains. The Gunsmith kept one eye on their back trail and the other eye on the Arabian's give-away right front foot.

TEN

The tall, hatchet-faced gunman stared so hard that Sheriff Rudd grew uncomfortable and looked off into the kitchen. "Lance, is this where Clint Adams fired from?"

"I told you it was! Why are we hanging around here anyway? That bitch and Adams are putting tracks between us right now. We may never find them if their trail goes cold."

"We'll find them," the sheriff vowed. "I've got an Apache tracker that will follow them to hell and back."

Lance didn't relax. "My dead partner ain't going to take much comfort in that."

"Your partner is history," the sheriff said quietly. "When it came time to dance, he was a little slow, and that's nobody's fault but his own."

"You're all heart, Rudd. But the thing of it is, I'm going after them now. You and your Apache can do whatever the hell you want."

"Suit yourself," Rudd said. "But it would be better if we rode together."

"You're a sheriff. What about Silver City? I can't imagine that folks around here would be all that happy about you chasing off after that Spanish gold."

"I'll stay the sheriff until we find that gold, and then I'll become the *ex*-sheriff. They elected me; if they're unhappy, they can go ahead and try to fire me. I really don't give much of a good gawddamn."

"Why not resign now?"

"Because," Rudd said, "if we take up the trail and I'm still wearing this badge, the law stays on my side. You can become my deputy. That way, we can shoot Adams on sight and still be on the right side of the law. If the trail runs long and hard, we can even get other marshals and sheriffs to help us out. Keeping this badge has a lot of big advantages, and I mean to use 'em for all they're worth."

The lean six-footer smiled coldly. "I just can't imagine me becoming a deputy."

"Why not?"

"Hell, Rudd! I've *shot* deputies."

The sheriff nodded stiffly. "Listen. Just trust me on this and do things my way. If I resign and we go after Adams and that girl, then we're nothing more than gold seekers. But if we are wearing badges, we can get any help we might need."

Lance patted his gun. "I won't need any help," he said confidently. "In fact, I'd like it better if you and your Apache tracker would just stay the hell out of my way. I'll find Adams and that prospector's daughter and take care of business."

"Sure," Rudd said sarcastically. "And then I'd never see that Spanish gold. Uh-uh. We're in this together. You may not realize it yet, Lance, but when you ride with the power of the law pinned to your chest, it makes a big difference."

Lance scoffed, but the sheriff chose to ignore him and said, "You search the front room and parlor, I'll take the bedroom and kitchen."

"What are we searching for?"

"Any letter, map, or written document that might give us a clue as to where they're heading."

"I'll be looking for money, jewelry, or valuables, and I'll bet you will too, *Sheriff*."

Rudd's cheeks reddened. "Just do what I say."

"All right," Lance said, "but I'd rather search the girl's bedroom."

"No."

"Why not?"

The sheriff didn't have a good answer, so he growled, "Suit yourself. I'll take the front room."

"She's a good-lookin' woman," Lance said. "I caught an eyeful of her yesterday over at the general store. I'd like to see what kind of underpants she wears. I bet she wears 'em lacy and perfumed."

"Jesus!" Rudd hissed. "Just keep your mind on what we're here for!"

But Lance wasn't listening. "I'll bet she's wanting another man since her husband got killed. When we catch up with her and Adams, reckon I'll teach her what a real man can do for a love-starved woman."

Rudd's jaw muscles tightened, and it was all he could do to hold his tongue. He didn't like or even trust Lance, but the man was a professional bounty hunter and a battle-tested gunman. Lance was the kind that would be useful when it came to a showdown and would be a match for Adams. At least, that was what Rudd was hoping.

Twenty minutes later, the sheriff was convinced that there was nothing in the house that would help them find the Spanish treasure. He walked into the bedroom to find Lance stuffing his pockets with Annie's silk underpants.

"What the hell are you doing? Put them back!" Rudd cried with outrage.

"Shut up," Lance said. "I told you that woman had an itchy bottom and liked nice underwear. I can trade these silk panties to the whores for their favors."

Rudd was disgusted. If he hadn't really needed a fast gun on his side against the likes of Clint Adams, he would never even have considered hooking up with the man in the first place.

"Let's go," the sheriff said.

"Where's this Apache you're plannin' to take along?"

"He lives a couple of miles outside of town."

"I don't like Indians," Lance said. "I like pretty young squaws, but that's all. You ever beat the blankets on an Indian girl, Sheriff?"

Rudd's cheeks warmed. "No."

"You should try one! Maybe this Apache has a sister or something that would take it in trade for one of these silk panties."

"You make me sick," Rudd said, turning on his heel and heading out the door.

A quarter of an hour later, Rudd was tacking a note of explanation on the door of his office, stating that a man had been killed and he was on the trail of the murderer, Clint Adams. In a hasty afterthought, Rudd added: Look for the body around town and have it planted at the county's expense.

"Here," Rudd said, flipping a badge to Lance. "I hereby make you a Silver City deputy."

"Do I draw any pay for it?"

"No, you just get to wear that badge and shoot Adams down on sight with the blessing of the law."

"Sounds good," Lance said, pinning the badge on his chest and checking his six-gun. He looked to the east and said, "Sun will be comin' up over them mountains any minute now, Sheriff. I'd guess Adams and that girl got a good three-hour head start on us. Seems to me like we don't have time to waste goin' to find no Apache tracker."

"Don't start trying to do my job," Rudd said, jamming a rifle into his saddle boot. "Manto is worth whatever time it takes to talk him into joining us."

"I ain't beggin' no Apache to ride with me."

"Then I'll do the beggin'," the sheriff said. "Manto won't come along if he doesn't think there's some pretty good money in it for him."

"How you going to convince him of that?"

Rudd reached into his pocket and pulled out a Spanish coin. He held it up to the dying starlight. "I took this off old Abe Morton when he was drunk and sick in my jail. I wouldn't let him out until he gave it to me."

"Damn!" Lance's eyes widened. "Mind if I take a closer look at that?"

"Yeah," the sheriff said, turning it back and forth and watching it flash, "as a matter of fact, I do. But there's a lot more of these waiting for us at the end of the trail. Maybe thousands."

Lance licked his lips. "Let's git!"

The sheriff mounted his horse and reined away. He spurred his mount into an easy gallop and did not stop until he reached an old shack several miles out of town. The shack was half wickiup, with a horse corral off to one side holding three handsome geldings that grew excited when they saw the new arrivals. A big dog was chained beside the front door, and its hackles were raised, its teeth bared.

"He don't look too friendly," Lance said.

"He'll tear your throat out if Manto gives the order," Rudd said. "I've seen what happened to a fella who tried to sneak in here and steal Manto's horses. It wasn't pretty."

"He ever comes at me, he'll eat lead."

"If you shoot the dog, you'll have to kill the Apache, and that wouldn't be easy."

"Maybe not for you," Lance growled, squinting into the rising sun. "I don't see no sign of a squaw."

"Manto's woman will stay inside until we go away." Rudd cupped his hands to his mouth and shouted. "Manto! It's Sheriff Rudd. Come on out of there. We need to talk!"

Before the call died against the hills, the Apache stepped out of the shack cradling a Winchester rifle. Though the morning air was cold, the Apache was bare-chested and barefooted. He was of average height, but very powerfully built with broad, heavily muscled shoulders, a thick neck, and a flat, impassive face.

"He looks like he'd slit your damned throat for a dollar," Lance said under his breath.

"Wrong," the sheriff whispered. "He'd slit both our throats for two bits."

"Then what the hell are we . . . ?"

"Manto," the sheriff called out, "I need a tracker!"

The Apache said nothing but waited until his guests

rode closer and the sheriff continued. "A killer and his lady friend escaped and rode into the mountains. The woman's horse has a bar shoe. It will be easy to pick up their trail."

"Then why do you need Manto?"

"I think that their trail will be long and the journey hard," Rudd said. "And I'm willing to pay you well."

"How much?"

Again, Rudd pulled out the Spanish coin, only this time, he tossed it to the impassive Indian, who caught and inspected it, then bit it.

"How many?"

"Enough to keep you in ponies and ammunition for the rest of your natural life."

"Where they go?"

"To find more where that one came from."

"Manto," Lance interrupted, "they're getting away right now. We don't have time to sit here and talk you into comin' with us. So what's it gonna be?"

The Indian stared at Lance, and then his black eyes flicked to the sheriff in a silent question.

"He's my deputy," Rudd said in explanation.

Manto did not look impressed, but he did turn and go back into his shack and close the door.

"What the hell," Lance said, "let's get out of here."

"No," the sheriff replied. "I think he's coming."

A moment later, the Apache appeared, dragging a saddle, with a Colt and cartridge belt looped over one shoulder.

"He *is* coming," Rudd said with obvious relief.

"Makes no difference to me," Lance growled. "So long as he understands the difference between a red man and a white man."

"And that is?"

"The red man sucks hind tit."

Rudd opened his mouth as if to say something, but then he changed his mind.

"If you've got something to say, then just spit it out!" Lance growled.

"All right," the sheriff said. "I think we're in for enough problems without you and Manto getting into a fight."

"I'll leave him alone," Lance said. "Just as long as he shows respect and knows where his place is."

"Oh, don't worry about that," Rudd said. "Manto knows exactly where his place is in the grand scheme of things."

"You sound like a damned Indian lover to me."

"I'm not," the sheriff protested. "But until we find that gold and take care of Adams, I want to make damn sure that we all work together. We need Manto for tracking, and we need to keep a peace between us."

"Sure," Lance said with a tight grin. "But before we leave, what's his squaw look like? Is she young or pretty?"

"She's both. But if you make a move for that shack, Manto will kill you, if his dog doesn't do it first."

Lance's grin dissolved into a sneer. "Shit, Rudd! You *are* a damned Indian lover!"

The sheriff reined his horse away, too disgusted to speak.

ELEVEN

They left the Apache's wickiup and started into the forest, Manto in the lead, followed by the sheriff and then Lance. They had traveled less than a mile when Lance suddenly reined in his horse and exclaimed, "Shit! I left my saddlebags back at that wickiup!"

"To hell with them," the sheriff growled.

"I gotta go back for them," Lance insisted. "I got my spare ammunition and all my things in those bags, including a bottle of whiskey."

"We don't need any whiskey," the sheriff argued. "Not until we've killed Adams and gotten our hands on that Spanish gold."

"You may not need any whiskey," Lance said, "but I do. Rudd, you can wait here or ride on. Either way, I'll catch up with you inside an hour or two."

"I don't think that would be a good idea," the sheriff said. "Besides, you were the one that kept saying we had to hurry along before the tracks went too cold."

"Listen," Lance spat, "I've also got a gun in those saddlebags and I'm not going to leave 'em behind.

They're hanging over a log where I was sitting while
we waited for the Apache. And I'm going to get 'em—
now."

Without waiting for further argument, Lance reined
his horse around and started back. Manto looked at the
sheriff and started to follow, but the sheriff reined his
horse sharply to block the Apache's path.

"I need you to help us find the tracks that will lead
us to that Spanish gold."

"I don't trust him."

"Neither do I," the sheriff said. "Are you still living
with Tekwa?"

"Yeah."

"Good," the sheriff said with a cold grin. "It ought to
be interesting."

Manto studied their back trail and weighed his need
to please the sheriff and find the Spanish gold against
his need to ride back and make sure that the bad white
was really interested in his missing saddlebags.

"Let's go," the sheriff said. "Time is wasting."

Finally, Manto reined his horse back onto the trail.
He kicked the horse forward and continued on through
the forest, his expression dark and brooding as he tried
to pull his thoughts back to the work that lay ahead.

Lance pushed his horse through the heavy forest at
a steady, ground-eating trot. His mind was on Manto's
squaw, and he was smiling with lustful anticipation.
When Lance came to the clearing and could see the
wickiup, he dismounted and retrieved his saddlebags,
which he then tied back in place.

He removed his battered gray Stetson, smoothed his

long, black, thinning hair, then replaced his hat and absently hitched up his dirty pants.

Manto's big dog was already growling deep in its throat. Lance did not even bother with the beast, but drew his six-gun and put two slugs through its chest. The dog kicked furiously in death, its fangs still bared as blood poured from its mouth.

"Woman! You know what I'm here for," he shouted as he approached the wickiup. "Come on out."

When there was no answer, Lance stepped over the still-kicking dog, reared back, and booted the door open. "Woman?"

There was no answer, so Lance leaned forward and peered inside. It was very black, and he couldn't see a damned thing. But he heard a sound and smiled as he stood framed in the doorway. "Hell, woman, don't be afraid. I'll treat you good."

"Go away," Tekwa said in a thick, guttural voice.

"Not until we've had ourselves some fun. I got money, if you ain't too ugly."

"Go away."

"Here," he said, digging into his pants. "I got a dollar. Look."

The Apache woman made no sound. Growing impatient, Lance removed his hat. "Honey, I can't see shit in there. Step outside so I can get a fair look at what I'm gonna be payin' for."

Another long silence brought a scowl to Lance's face. "I got to get back to your man and the sheriff before too long. There's no time to play games."

Lance waited for a reply, and when it came, it was in the form of a metallic click of a hammer being cocked.

Lance threw himself forward as an orange blossom of flame stabbed out of the darkness toward him. He rolled into the darkness, his own gun filling his hand and answering with fire. Lance heard a sharp gasp of pain, and he lunged forward, landing on the muscular and musky-smelling body of the Indian woman.

"Dammit!" he shouted, slapping her face once forward and once backward. "Why are you makin' this so hard?"

The woman screeched like a cat and clawed at his face. Lance ducked his head against her buckskins, feeling the large mounds of her heaving breasts. His passion soared, and Lance's hand fumbled for the hem of her skirt, trying to drag it up around her hips.

"You're a damned hellion," he panted.

For a moment, the Indian woman went limp, and Lance thought that he had broken her will to fight. But then, she screamed and batted at his face.

"Why you . . ." He raised his fist to strike her but felt a horrible pain fill his stomach.

"Ahhh!" Lance screamed, as a crimson veil dropped across his bulging eyes. His hand went to his belly, and only then did he realize that a knife was buried deep in his guts. He felt the woman's hand knotted tightly over the wooden handle, and when he tried to pull them both away from his belly, Lance had no strength.

The woman said something in Apache, and her wrist twisted back and forth, screwing the blade of the knife deeper and deeper into his guts.

Lance squirmed like a worm on a barb and cursed the Apache woman. He rolled away, feeling the knife still twisting in his gut, and managed to crawl to the door of the wickiup, where he stuck his head out into the sun. His eyelids beat at the sky like the wings of a butterfly, and his jaw dropped as he tried to drag in fresh air and keep the darkness from blanketing his mind.

The Indian woman landed squarely on his back, driving the blade to his spine. She grabbed his hair and yanked his head back. Lance caught a dying vision of Tekwa. She would have been pretty, except that she was missing her nose. He blinked, knowing that she had suffered the Apache punishment for adultery. He saw that one of her sleeves was saturated with fresh blood where his bullet had creased her arm.

Lance tried to speak, but there was no strength left even for words. The woman spat in his face and dropped it into the dirt, then she stepped over his body and went to wash her wound in a nearby stream.

The Apache woman removed her clothes, then stepped into the cold mountain stream. She was short, squat, but still supple and muscular. Squatting so that the water came to her full breasts, Tekwa began to wash her buckskins free of the white man's smell and her own blood. Overhead, a blue jay scolded her in a raucous voice. Tekwa looked up at the bird, her dark eyes picking the blue jay out of the backdrop of forest.

When her buckskins were clean, she hung them over a willow branch and then laid herself down on a warm rock to dry in the sun. She would have to saddle a horse and drag both the dog and the evil white man's body far off into the trees so that their smell of decay would not attract bears or cougars to her wickiup. But that would not take long or be difficult. She would first strip the man's body of valuables. He had a nice gun and a good horse and saddle.

Tekwa began to hum, for she was happy. Her arm would soon heal, and when Manto finally returned, he would be very pleased with their new possessions.

TWELVE

The Gunsmith reined Duke up and let the animal drink in the mountain stream. "Well, Annie," he said, turning to face the woman, "are you still sure that we're looking at the right mountain?"

"Yes," she replied. "See that massive pine tree jutting out from the face of that sheer cliff?"

"Uh-huh."

"That's pretty unusual, wouldn't you say?"

"I would."

"My father thought so too. He told me that it looked like . . . well, never mind."

The Gunsmith smiled; that single great pine looked like an erection. "So what do you suppose we ought to do now?"

"We ride to a place just under that tree and take a sighting due west."

"And what does that tell us?"

"We'll see another landmark."

"You want to tell me about it?"

"No," she said, "I'll tell you about it when I see it."

"Fair enough," the Gunsmith said. "But I'd expect the sun to be going down by the time we reach that cliff. This country is too rough to be riding around in the dark."

"I know. My father said that this stream comes boiling out of a place under that cliff. He camped there many a time."

"Any idea how far we still have to ride?"

"I'd say another two, maybe three days."

Clint was not surprised to hear this. Annie had been telling him from the start that the trail to the hidden Spanish treasure was long and difficult.

"I'll have to shoot a buck in another day or two. We're getting low on provisions."

"Whatever you have to do," Annie said, "do it."

The Gunsmith let Duke drink his fill, and then they continued on up the mountain, following a narrow, twisting trail. Clint could not imagine that the early Spaniards had struggled up into these high, inhospitable mountains centuries ago. Back then, this place had probably been crawling with ferocious grizzly bears. By now most all of them had been shot by the early trappers and prospectors.

"Can you imagine my father coming all the way out here?" Annie called from atop her Arabian mare. "He must have been crazy to come alone into this kind of country."

"He wasn't the first to prospect these mountains," Clint assured her. "And besides, maybe he had a partner."

"Never," Annie insisted. "The only company my father allowed when he went off searching for gold or silver was his burro. My father wasn't an especially sociable man, except when he was drinking. And even then he was apt to get into a fight."

"I've seen the type," Clint said. "Men who live by themselves seem to lose the ability to be sociable. When they come into a town, they're like fish out of water. They drink too much. After a few hours in some saloon swilling bad but expensive liquor, they either wind up in a fight or else spend the night in jail."

"You sound like a man talking from experience."

"I've been a lawman, if that's what you mean. And I guess because of it, I don't have much use for someone like Sheriff Rudd."

"He's worthless at best, dangerous at worst."

"Do you really think that he'd come after us?" Clint asked, remembering how eager Rudd had been to quit his job and join him on this treasure hunt.

"He's done it before."

"Why doesn't the town council fire him?"

"Because he's paid by the county, and he has influential friends at that level," Annie explained. "And also, he's let it be known through his rougher friends that any attempt to replace him would result in bloodshed."

"I see. And these friends, they're a dangerous bunch?"

"Rough is much too mild a term, Clint. They're ruthless killers who would do anything for a dollar. You can bet that Rudd has dangled the promise of Spanish gold before their eyes, and they are willing to get it at any price."

"Let's just hope that they never find our trail," Clint said. "I'd like to keep your mare's hoof wrapped, but in this rocky country, even leather wears through after a few miles."

They finally reached the base of the high, sheer cliff with the distinctive tree jutting out from its face about seventy feet overhead. Almost directly underneath the tree, the underground river appeared. It was cold and delicious. The Gunsmith dismounted and unsaddled his horse. Annie did the same, and they hobbled both animals and let them graze on the sweet meadow grass.

"These horses are worn down by all the hard riding that we've been doing," Annie said, "but you have to admit that my mare is getting stronger every day."

"She is," Clint agreed. "She's quite a horse. At first, I wasn't very impressed. But I was wrong about Arabians. They're damned tough horses."

"You can say that again," Annie added. "I'm going to gather firewood, then we'll boil some potatoes and heat up the last of that old jerky we brought from Silver City."

"Maybe I'd better try and drop a nice young buck this evening," Clint suggested.

Annie watched him pull his Winchester from its saddle boot. "Whatever you think. I just figured that you might want to avoid the sound of a shot."

"If we're being tracked, and they're close enough to hear a rifle shot, then we might as well make a stand right here where we have our backs protected against this cliff and we've got meat, grass, and water."

"I guess you're right," she said, not sounding very sure. "What you're saying is that it would be better to fight here than to be overtaken and ambushed by surprise out on some exposed trail or ridge."

"Exactly," Clint said as he checked his rifle and then studied the dying sun. "Annie, I think it would be best if you didn't forage off into the woods but stayed close to camp while I'm gone hunting."

"All right," she said. "There's deadwood right over there at the base of the tree. And I've already located an old camp fire ring, probably the one used by my father."

"Good." Clint looked up at the rock wall. He thought that any smoke from their fire would strike the wall and dissipate nicely. "Keep the fire small and the coals hot. I can almost taste the roasted venison."

As he started to leave, Annie said, "I suppose you're every bit as good with that Winchester as you are with a six-gun?"

"No," he admitted, "but I can generally hit what I aim for, especially when my belly is growling."

Annie laughed, and the sound was pleasing enough so that Clint said, "You have a nice laugh and a pretty smile. You should use both of them more often."

"I will," she said, "once we have our gold deposited in a bank and we are safely out of these mountains."

"Spanish gold may not make either one of us happy, Annie."

"It will go a long ways toward helping," she said. "And so will fresh meat. The idea of eating any more of that old jerky and those mushy potatoes isn't very appealing."

"Right." Clint headed off across the meadow as the sun dipped below the western peaks.

Moving stealthily across the meadow and into the trees, Clint knew that he had less than half an hour to hunt. Any longer than that, and it would be dark. With that in mind, he walked rapidly downriver while trying to keep as quiet as possible. The Gunsmith recalled that they had ridden past a smaller meadow less than a half mile downriver, and he was optimistic that he would find deer grazing there in the fading light of day. At the very worst, it would give him an opportunity to survey a little of their back trail.

When Clint came to the edge of the forest, he stopped and leaned close to a pine tree. The light was quickly dying, but he was in luck because there were eight deer grazing on the lush meadow grass. For a few moments, Clint forgot about the deer as his eyes surveyed the trail and the ridges for sign of any pursuit. He used almost five precious minutes studying the lower mountainside, and while an entire army could have been hiding behind rocks and trees, the Gunsmith felt sure that he and Annie were alone.

The Gunsmith did not select the largest buck, a fine four-pointer. Instead, he chose a smaller two-point buck that would be easier to pack. Raising his rifle, he took a deep, steadying breath and then aimed for a spot close behind the buck's foreleg. When he squeezed the trigger, the buck dropped like a stone, and the rest of the herd darted into the trees quicker than a man could lever his rifle and get off a second shot.

It took the Gunsmith less than a quarter of an hour to gut and prepare the buck. Rather than try to pack it over his shoulders, Clint decided that he would simply drag its carcass back to camp. The light was almost gone, and he was nearly dizzy from hunger.

Clint used a leather thong to sling his rifle over his left shoulder, then he began to drag the carcass back upriver. He was tired, famished, but feeling good. The light of Annie's small camp fire was a beacon, and it brought him swiftly back to their camp.

"I heard your shot," she said. "Nice work."

"Thanks," Clint said, retrieving his knife and getting busy slicing a few long strips of venison for their fire.

In less than fifteen minutes they were devouring the hot, juicy venison from the tips of green willow switches. Both he and Annie ate their fill, and neither one of them even looked at the potatoes.

The stars filled the inky heavens, and the Gunsmith realized he was very weary as he stretched out on his bedroll.

"No sign of pursuit, I take it?"

"None at all."

"Good! But I still think that they'll be coming."

"If they do, we'll manage," Clint promised, closing his eyes.

"Did you know that you snore?"

Clint opened his eyes. "Yep, but few women complain."

"I'll bet."

He rolled over to peer through the darkness at Annie. She was lying across the fire from him, where she seemed to feel safest. Clint didn't care, he had no interest in a woman who didn't want him in return. He and Annie were partners in this fortune hunt, no more, and no less. That was her firm statement, not his. But now, she had wakened him a little with her comment, and he wanted to know why.

"What does 'I'll bet' mean?"

"It just means that I'll bet that no women complained. When you pay women for their favors, they're hardly in a position to criticize you about snoring."

"For your information, Annie, I don't pay women," he said with an edge to his voice. "Never."

"Oh, really?"

"Yeah." Clint was annoyed. "Have you ever paid men for it, Annie?"

"What a stupid question! Up until you shot and killed my husband, I was married, remember?"

"Of course I do." Clint propped himself up on one elbow. "Listen, it's late and I'm tried. We've got another long ride tomorrow so let's go to sleep and quit playing games."

"I'm *not* playing games. I was just telling you that you snore, that's all. I don't know why you're making such a big deal out of that."

Clint sighed and placed his hat over his face. In a few minutes, he was drifting off to sleep. He didn't understand this woman and probably never would. Sure, she was a good-looking gal and he wished they could become better acquainted, but that wasn't about to happen so there was little point in worrying about anything except that damned Spanish gold.

"Good night, Clint."

He raised his hat. She'd never said good night to him before. It was nice. "Good night," he replied.

And then, he really did fall asleep.

THIRTEEN

At first the Gunsmith thought that the roar he heard was the sound of the river pouring out from the base of the mountain, but he quickly realized that this was not the case. Clint snapped his eyes open and saw the outline of a huge grizzly bear.

"Annie!" Clint hissed, feeling his mouth go cotton-dry with fear.

She was sleeping soundly and did not hear him as the bear moved toward her, blood dripping from its jowls from the deer carcass the beast had been feasting on.

"Annie!"

Clint slowly sat up and reached out for his rifle. The grizzly growled low in its throat and twisted in Clint's direction, eyes gleaming red in the firelight. When Clint levered a shell into the breech, the bear lifted on its hind legs and growled louder, startling Annie.

"Clint?"

"Don't move!" he shouted, kneeling as the rifle came to his shoulder. "Annie, stay dead still."

The grizzly swung back at the Gunsmith and dropped to its hind legs. Clint wasn't positive, but he thought the animal was about to charge. He wasn't at all sure if his puny .30-.30 carbine would stop the bear, but he was ready to find out.

With a deep roar building in its throat, the grizzly did charge. Fortunately, it had to circle around the fire, and that took another second or two. By then Clint was furiously working his rifle, trying to hit the bear's vital organs with each shot. The grizzly took the bullets in stride, and it was not until the third bullet struck it just under the jaw that the huge beast faltered. Clint was on his feet, ramming shot after shot into the dying grizzly. The bear lurched forward but toppled when struck by the Gunsmith's fifth bullet.

But even then the grizzly wasn't finished. It rolled in agony, then somehow managed to get back on its feet in a dying, demented charge that carried it into the Gunsmith with all the force of a rushing locomotive. Clint smelled burning hair as he fired the last bullet, and the monster collapsed on him in a quivering heap. For a few terrified seconds, the Gunsmith struggled, and then he lost consciousness.

When he awoke, he was covered with blood and thought for sure that he was dying. He felt crushed and wondered if the bear had gotten to Annie.

"Clint?"

He looked up and saw Annie hovering over him, silhouetted against a brilliant sunrise. It seemed to Clint as if he was staring at an angel framed by a heaven of lavender and lace.

"Annie, are you all right?" he croaked, reaching up to touch her face.

"I'm fine," she whispered, wiping his brow with a damp rag. "I thought you were a goner. I don't know how I ever dragged you out from under that terrible beast."

"I don't either," he said with genuine amazement. "How badly am I hurt?"

"I couldn't find anything other than some scrapes and scratches. Maybe you have broken ribs, but I couldn't tell by examination."

The Gunsmith was resting on his bedroll and covered with Annie's blankets. He reached down and fingered his rib cage, and only then did he realize that he was naked. Pressing each rib, he checked them off one by one until he was satisfied that none were either broken or cracked.

"Are they all right?" she asked, concern etched deep into her pretty face.

"I . . . I don't know," he hedged. "Here, see what you think about this one."

Before Annie realized it, he had her soft hand moving down his chest to his lower rib, and then he pulled her hand even farther south. Annie's face was inches from his own as her eyes grew wide with surprise.

"What are you doing?" she whispered as he eased her trembling fingers around his stiffening manhood.

"You know what I'm doing," he said in a husky voice as he slipped his other arm around her neck and pulled her down on top of him.

For a moment, Annie made a pretense of struggling, but then their lips met and a fire passed through them. Her hand closed tightly around his rod, and Clint felt her tongue probe his mouth. A wildness seized them both, and before Annie could even think to form a protest, Clint was reaching under her blouse, fondling her breasts and driving her into a sweet ecstasy.

"Oh, damn you!" she panted, kicking her boots over the dead grizzly.

Clint just grinned before his mouth found her full and eager nipples. Moments later, she was squirming passionately under him and guiding his stiff rod into her eager body. Annie's eyes were wide open and so was the moist place between her legs. Clint plunged into her. Annie sighed happily and wrapped her legs around his lean hips.

"I knew we'd come to this," she told him in a rush. "I knew it!"

"I didn't," he confessed, hips pumping in a slow but powerful circle. "Actually, I was hoping it would, but I didn't dare build my own expectations."

"And you were too much of a gentleman to force yourself on me and take advantage."

"Maybe," he said, lips pulling back from his teeth. "But right now we're not worried about being a lady or a gentleman, are we, Annie?"

"No," she breathed, grabbing his buttocks and fiercely pulling him deeper inside. "And this is a whole lot better for my money."

The Gunsmith thought so too. He felt as if he were the luckiest man alive to have escaped being mauled and killed by the grizzly only to awaken with a girl like Annie at his side. And now that she was under him, urging his body to satisfy her body, it really was like being in heaven.

"I'm crazy to be doing this," she breathed. "It's going to screw up everything between us."

"Why?"

"Because this feels so damned good we won't want to keep riding."

Clint laughed and felt a fire kindling inside him. "We'll ride. We *are* riding."

"This is not what I meant and you know it!"

"It's better," he said, kissing her mouth and then pulling away to watch her eyes glaze with pleasure as his body made her body twitch and buck. "Admit it."

"No!" she squealed, digging her fingernails into his buttocks and pulling him deeper and deeper.

"Admit it," he teased, "or I'll drive you completely out of your lovely little mind, then turn you loose out here in the wilderness a satisfied but crazed woman."

"All right, I admit it! Now quit talking and please drive me mad!"

The Gunsmith was ready, willing, and able. They forgot about the dead bear and the men that hunted them like a pack of bloodthirsty dogs. They forgot about everything except the fire in their blood, and when they both lost control, they howled at the rising sun like a couple of coyotes.

Afterward, Annie looked deep into his eyes. "I don't suppose I measure up to Sally."

"Why not?"

"She had a lot more experience."

"You're just as good and every bit as eager. I wouldn't trade you for anyone."

"You mean that?" Annie sat up and stared hard at him, as if she could read a lie.

"Yeah," he said, reaching out and pulling her back down to his side. "I really mean it."

"And when we find my father's Spanish treasure, what then?"

"We take it to Santa Fe or some other town and bank it."

"And then?"

Clint smiled. "And then I don't have the foggiest idea. I'm going to be rich, and you're going to be rich. Isn't that enough?"

"No. Clint, you said that money can't buy happiness. You meant that, didn't you?"

"Yes, but . . ."

"I think we could make each other very happy. I think that we could make love in every country in the world and do it twice on Sunday."

"Why should we do it all over the world?"

"Because I've always wanted to travel and see other countries. Don't you?"

"I don't know," he said with amusement. "I'm pretty happy roaming around the West. It suits me just fine."

Annie's brow knitted, and she played with the hair on the Gunsmith's chest, twirling it about her index finger. "Well then, perhaps we could just buy ourselves a big ranch someplace and raise a large family."

"Whoa!" Clint exclaimed. "Don't you think we're moving a little fast?"

"There's no saying how much time any of us have," she reminded him. "People are always dying suddenly. There are no guarantees."

"That's right," he said, rolling over and entering her one last time before they left this place and continued on their treasure hunt. "And that's why we're doing what brings us the most pleasure right now."

She giggled and laid her hands on his buttocks. "Aren't you ever going to get enough of me?"

"I mean to find out."

"Good," she said, hugging him tightly, "because I *know* I'll never get enough of you."

Clint lost himself in her again, and when he finally came, they were panting and gasping and he found that he was damned near empty.

"We've got to saddle up and ride," he said, rolling sideways. "And we'll be taking not only venison, but also bear meat."

"Yes," Annie agreed with a contented sigh before she closed her eyes and fell into an exhausted sleep.

Clint studied the huge bear and then padded over to his buck, which was half-devoured. Maybe, he thought, glancing back over his shoulder at Annie, it would be good to rest for a full day. The horses were tired and growing footsore.

"Who are you kidding?" the Gunsmith said to himself with a smile as he scratched and wondered how soon he could make love to Annie again.

FOURTEEN

"That's it!" Annie cried.

The Gunsmith stood up in his stirrups. "What? The spot where we can finally dig for the buried treasure?"

"No, of course not," she replied. "It's the landmark my father described. Here, look on this piece of map that Father gave you. See the stream and the fork where it plunges down into the Gila?"

Clint peered at the map where she was pointing. "Sure, I see it, but there are hundreds of streams that flow into the Gila. How are we supposed to know that he had this particular one in mind?"

"Because. You see this line?"

Clint squinted. "Barely."

"Well, that represents that lightning-struck tree. He told me to look for one that was charred and splintered at the top. He said it looked like the talons of a raven."

Clint studied the twisted, burned-out pine tree that had probably been hit at least ten years earlier. "It is pretty distinctive," he agreed.

"You bet it is!" Annie said, unable to hide her excitement as she spurred her Arabian mare forward.

"How many of these damned landmarks are we going to have to find before we finally get to that buried Spanish gold?"

"Who said it was buried?"

Clint was taken aback by that and spurred his own horse forward to catch the young woman. "Wait a minute, Annie. You said it was *buried* treasure."

"No I didn't. Not ever," she countered. "I said that it was hidden, and I suppose that it might even be buried, but I doubt that very much."

"Well, why not?"

"Because," Annie said, reining her horse up beside the charred pine tree and dismounting, "my father was smart, tough, and he would have been a good prospector except for one thing."

"What, his drinking?"

"All right," she said, handing the Gunsmith her reins. "Except for *two* things. The drinking and the fact that he hated hard work."

Clint frowned. "I don't see what that . . ."

"Despite years of prospecting, my father hated a pick and shovel. He'd pick a little here and there but never really get serious. And as for shovels, he called them a farmer's tools."

"I still don't get it."

"He was lazy. *Very* lazy. After he found that gold, it would be like him to hide or leave it in a cave rather than move and rebury it."

"But you don't know for sure?"

Annie looked away and said. "When we find the last landmark, we'll know for certain."

Clint was exasperated. "I get it. You still aren't going to tell me about the last landmark."

"Until we find the next one, what would be the point?"

"There's *two* more?"

"Yes."

"How far from here?"

"I expect to reach the treasure in three days," Annie said, facing west and sighting on the tree where its massive old trunk had splintered. "Look where I'm pointing."

"Why don't you just tell me?"

"All right, we follow this river, and I think that we'll find a landslide with lots of quartz and even a little turquoise."

"And then?"

"Then we look for a sign that my father told me about."

Clint nodded. He'd learned enough by now to understand that there was no prodding Annie. She'd reveal everything to him in her own sweet but maddening time.

"There's only a couple of hours of daylight left, Annie. Maybe we should camp here for the night."

She laughed. "Be honest, Clint, you just want to jump me, don't you?"

"You're a lot more fun to ride than this gelding."

"I should hope so. But I think we ought to push on awhile before we make camp. My father said that he had often panned gold where this stream joins the Gila. I thought that if we had an hour or two tonight and in the morning, we could try and pan a few dollars worth of nuggets."

"That's not one of my specialties," Clint said without enthusiasm. "I've never been lucky that way."

"Well, one night when my father was drunk, he showed me a poke of gold dust and nuggets, and he swore that this stream was rich with placer ore."

"What do we need it for if we find the Spanish gold?"

"Maybe we won't find our treasure. And if we don't, wouldn't it be nice to at least have a poke of gold dust to pay for supplies, a room, and a meal when we finally return to civilization?"

"I suppose it would," he had to admit. "But we don't even have gold pans."

"Our tin dinner plates will do. Don't forget that you're talking to a prospector's daughter. So if you don't know how to work a pan, I'll be more than happy to show you."

"I'll just bet you would."

By the time they reached the Gila River, Clint still wasn't excited about the idea of prospecting. They quickly made camp, then got ready to try their luck.

"I'm going to take off my boots and socks," Annie said, picking up her pan and hurrying over to a sandbar near the confluence of the stream and the river. "And I'd advise you to do the same. You also might want to hang your six-gun on something."

"Not a chance," Clint said. "The last time I did that was when Deke and his friend caught me off guard while I was trying to untangle a whale of a trout."

"I see." Annie shrugged. "Well then, if you feel more comfortable, wear your gun and boots. It's all the same to me. Just roll up your sleeves and bring your tin plate." Annie glanced up at the dying sun. "We've got about an hour to work this stream, and I expect you to do your share."

Clint was tired, and the last thing he wanted to do was pan for gold. But Annie was right—they did need some spending money, and if this stream was a fluid gold mine, then it wouldn't hurt to give it a fair try.

"No, no," Annie said, glancing over at the Gunsmith, who was up to his knees in water and sloshing a lot of gravel out of his dinner plate. "You need to back into more shallow water. And don't take such a big scoop of sand and gravel. A small amount will work better."

"You want to try it with two plates?"

"No. Now watch."

Annie demonstrated how Clint should scoop up a little bit of sand and gravel, then work it just under the surface of the stream in a circular motion that struck Clint as being very sensuous.

"You'll get the motion," she said, looking up as she demonstrated.

"I guess I will," he replied, feeling an erection starting to build.

Suddenly, Annie stared at her tin plate. "Look! A nugget!"

Clint forgot about his amorous intentions. He hurried over to stare at the contents of Annie's plate and saw a nugget about the size of a ladybug. It had a dull gleam and was easily distinguishable from the rest of the sand and gravel.

"Well, I'll be damned!" Clint said. "A nugget that size is probably worth five dollars."

"At least," Annie said excitedly. "If we could find a dozen or so like this one, we'd have nearly a hundred dollars."

"Maybe it's just beginner's luck," he cautioned. "But you've made a believer out of me."

Clint went right to work with his tin plate, and when Annie squealed again that she'd found another similar sized nugget, that made him all the more determined to find one of his own.

The Gunsmith was rewarded less than fifteen minutes later when he found a potato-shaped nugget, the biggest yet. "Annie, would you look at this!"

He slogged over to her and plucked it out of his plate, but the damned thing was slippery and scooted out between his thumb and forefinger to vanish back into the stream. Clint dove for the nugget and came up wet and empty.

"Dammit! I lost 'er!"

"Don't worry," Annie consoled. "There's bound to be more."

"Yeah, but that one was worth at least ten dollars."

"Stop bellyaching and keep panning," she ordered, working furiously against the fading light of day.

Clint hadn't been inflicted with gold fever since his youth, and he was surprised at how exciting panning gold could be when you actually found enough to make good money. In the space of another quarter hour, he found two more nuggets, both small, but bigger than the tiny specks of dust that most prospectors traded for goods, and probably worth two or three dollars each.

"Maybe our luck is finally starting to change," he said happily as they panned until it was too dark to tell the difference between ore and rock.

FIFTEEN

Sheriff Rudd was growing impatient. They had already lost a full day trying to pick up the Gunsmith's trial after he'd covered the Arabian's bar shoe, and now the trail was looping around in a big circle that made no sense at all. The sun was fading, and the sheriff checked his cinch, his mind clouded with worry.

"Manto, tell me what you think."

"I think this smart man," the Apache replied. "But maybe he lost."

"Naw," the sheriff grunted, heaving on his latigo leather so hard he made his horse grunt as the cinch bit deeper into its barrel. "They aren't lost. They're just following that damned map that the old man had on him when he was killed."

"Maybe map no good."

"Maybe," the sheriff agreed. "Could be that Abe is having the last laugh on all of us from hell."

"Horses tired."

"So are we, but we'll keep riding as long as the light holds," Rudd said, glancing up at the fading sun. "And

112

you know what I'm thinking?"

When the Apache didn't answer, Rudd continued, "I'm thinking that this trail can wind all over creation, but that it has to come back to the Gila River. I heard Abe talk about the Gila River and that Spanish gold, and I have to think that's where we'll find 'em."

The Apache said nothing. He would let the sheriff make the decisions and then have to live with them if they were wrong. He'd learned long ago that that was the best way for an Indian to avoid blame.

"I'm thinking about leaving this trail and striking out for the Gila, then following it west until we chance upon them or their trail," the sheriff said, looking at the Apache to see if his instincts were right.

Rudd waited for a response, but the Indian simply mounted his horse and sat. "Well?" he finally asked with some impatience. "What do you think?"

"Think we lose them tracks in those damn canyons," the Apache finally said.

"Yeah, there's a chance of that. But this country is so rough that we're not closing on them much, if any. Why, we could track them all the way to Tucson, Arizona, and then lose 'em to a stage line."

The sheriff sighed. "Manto," he said, reaching his decision, "we've got to close on 'em quicker. I know that you're doing your best, but this rough country is holding us up, and it ain't helping that Adams keeps wading up every damn stream and river he can find in order to shake us off his trail."

"He knows that we are coming. And there are others behind us."

Rudd's jaw sagged, and his head twisted around to stare up their back trail. "You seen 'em?"

"No."

"Well then . . ."

"I seen their dust yesterday."

The sheriff felt his stomach muscles tighten with anxiety. "Any idea how many?"

"At least four," Manto said. "Traveling fast."

The sheriff understood what the Apache was saying. While he and Manto had been held back by Clint Adams's cleverness, anyone who was pursuing them would not be hindered.

"What do you figure we ought to do?"

"Ambush them," Manto said without hesitation. "Find high place and shoot them from their horses. Best way of taking care of trouble."

"Yeah, it would be, but we can't afford to wait around and lose another day or two."

"Catch us tomorrow," Manto announced with absolute certainty. "Kill tomorrow."

"All right," Rudd said. "I know that you're a pretty good man with a rifle, and I can hit what I aim for nine times out of ten. But if there are a bunch more than you think, we're the ones that are going to be in for a surprise."

"Manto find good place. Kill them all."

Rudd nodded and climbed onto his weary horse. "I wish you would have told me about us being followed before now," he groused.

"You worry too much about everything," Manto said. "Why worry about more?"

Rudd glared at the stoic Apache. He didn't like Manto, but he trusted the Indian. They'd been on more than one manhunt, and Rudd had learned that while the Apache was not infallible, he was right a whole lot

more often than he was wrong. He'd also learned that
the Indian had a sixth sense that was indefinable but
very real. Manto could also see better in the dark
than any white man and his sense of smell was far
keener.

"Tell me this," Rudd said. "How do you think that
Tekwa killed Lance?"

Manto's black eyes clouded with anger, and when he
spoke, his voice was like a lash. "It does not matter! I
hope Tekwa kill that man slow with knife so he scream.
But maybe dog tear out throat."

"You never had any doubt that Lance would get to
your woman, did you?"

The Apache did not even think it worthwhile to
answer the question.

"Let's go," Rudd said, mounting his horse and waiting for Manto to lead off down the trail. "We're heading
for the Gila River and to hell with the tracks. We'll pick
them up again on the Gila."

Manto did not look completely convinced, but Rudd
did not give a damn. The sheriff was, by nature, a
worrier, and now he had another big worry on his
mind—the men following them. No doubt they were
trying to keep out of sight and hoping to make their
move for the Spanish gold when everyone else had
killed each other off. That was obviously why they were
hanging back. Well, the sheriff thought, tomorrow they
would get more than they bargained for.

The sheriff of Silver City and his Apache tracker
rode until after dark, then made a hurried and cold
camp. Expecting no attack, they did not bother to take
turns staying awake at night but slept well. In the

morning, the sheriff awoke stiff, cold, but rested. He and Manto did not speak as they broke camp and lined out for the Gila River some five or six miles away. They rode down through a narrow, rugged canyon, following an old game trail with a thousand switchbacks. In some places, the brush was so thick that they had to dismount and lead their horses and often use sticks to lift low-hanging branches so that their saddles would clear. It was slow and difficult work, and they did not break through the brush and stumble upon the Gila River until early afternoon.

The men and horses were thirsty and so tired from their hard travels that they slogged right into the water, collapsed, and drank their fill.

"There's grass here for the horses and probably plenty of wild game to shoot," the sheriff said, wanting nothing more than to get off his horse and rest.

"No," Manto said. "We kill men at sundown."

"Where?"

"Here."

The sheriff gazed around, not really wanting to face this gunfight and yet knowing he had to. The Gila was about fifty yards wide, not especially deep but quite swift. There was a lot of water and brush, and the visibility was diminished by the long, dark shadows cast by the surrounding cliffs.

"How do you think we ought to position ourselves?"

"There," the Apache said, pointing to a low pile of rocks not seventy feet from the trail they'd spilled off of to reach the water. "And over there."

Rudd followed the Apache's finger. "A cross fire, huh?"

Manto nodded. "We catch 'em good."

"And what if there are a lot more than four of 'em? What are we going to do then?"

Manto shrugged.

"No," Rudd said, "that ain't good enough. We'll hide our horses a little ways upriver. I'll wait down here in position, but I want you to hike back up the trail and get a glimpse of them. If there are more than four, I think we'd better keep moving."

Manto wasn't pleased, but he dipped his chin and handed over his reins. Taking a last drink of water and pulling his own rifle from its scabbard, the Apache vanished up the narrow game trail that they'd just descended.

Rudd lingered for about ten minutes alongside the Gila River. He wished that he were back in Silver City, maybe taking his pleasure with one of the saloon girls that he used on a frequent basis. And a little whiskey would go just fine. Rudd's stomach was growling, and he felt nervous. He'd killed men before and wasn't afraid of danger, only this time he was not sure how many men he would have to face and that uncertainty was pretty frightening.

"Come on, horses," he said, dragging them upriver and slogging through the shallows so that they would leave no tracks. He rounded a bend and found a good place in the rocks to tie the animals. Any sound they might make would be masked by the river.

Taking his own rifle and checking his gun even though he knew that it was ready for action, the sheriff hurried back downriver and took position in one of the ambushing places indicated by Manto. He squinted his eyes and stared up at the tall, silent cliffs all around. Dying in this stone coffin would not be to

his liking. If he were killed in this ambush, he knew
that Manto would not bother to bury him, nor would
the men who were tracking them. That meant his body
would soon be torn apart and devoured by wild animals.
That realization made Rudd's bowels churn so hard that
he had to relieve himself.

An hour slowly passed and then another, but there
was still no sign of the Apache. Sheriff Rudd kept
glancing from the trail to the cliffs and found no comfort in either view. But finally Manto did appear, and
the Indian came swiftly over to his side.

"How many?"

"Six."

"Six!" The sheriff cursed. "Dammit, even if we are
lucky enough to knock four of 'em down before they
can take cover, that will still leave two more to worry
about!"

"We kill. No problem."

"Two against six ain't odds to my liking, even if we
do have the element of surprise."

"Too late to run, Sheriff. Men come soon."

Rudd knew that the Apache was right. And besides,
the idea of being only a few hours ahead of the men
who were trailing them, waiting for their own chance
to pounce, was not a bit to Rudd's liking.

"All right," he said heavily. "Let's make war and try
to come out of this alive."

Manto must have thought that comment amusing,
because he laughed as he went to take his place in
ambush. Rudd could feel his heart pounding as he
waited. He strained to listen for the sound of a shod
hoof striking a rock, because he knew that he would
hear the six men before he would see them.

It was almost dusk when he finally heard the approaching riders and horses. Rudd gripped his rifle tightly and eased it down across a rock. He knew that Manto would probably take the first rider, figuring him for a tracker like himself. Rudd decided to take the second rider and then the fourth. After that, there would be a hard fight to kill the fifth and sixth men who would have time to dismount and take cover.

Manto had positioned himself well, and when the riders suddenly came abreast of him, his upper body popped up and he fired. The first rider took a bullet through his ear and never knew what hit him. Manto's second shot was right on the heels of Rudd's first shot, and two more riders tumbled off their frightened horses. They got lucky when a rearing horse tossed off the fourth man, and he landed hard, breaking his neck.

The two remaining riders were quick and smart. Instead of trying to control their horses and rein them around, both men threw themselves into the rocks. One of the men cried out in pain, but the other returned fire.

Rudd saw the Apache moving like a wraith through the brush to circle around behind the two surviving men. Manto would wait until he was right in their back pockets before he opened fire again.

"Sheriff!" the injured man cried. "It's me, Alan Potts! I'm hurt! We need to talk!"

Rudd knew Potts for what he was, a gunfighter and a worthless horse thief. "No deal!"

There was a curse and then a flurry of bullets. Rudd squatted low and returned a few more shots just to keep their minds on his position.

"Sheriff! It's me, Bill Tigert. Let us get our horses and we'll go away! Ain't no sense of anyone else dying. What do you say?"

"No deal!" Rudd shouted. "You boys came sneaking up my back trail, and you weren't there in case I ran into trouble. You were figuring to kill me and Manto."

"Call the damned Apache off!" Tigert begged. "Sheriff, we're surrendering to you."

"Then throw out your weapons."

"Potts snapped his leg when he landed. He's hurt real bad."

"Your guns!" Rudd ordered. "Throw them out now!"

The sheriff heard the two men arguing in the rocks. It was clear that Tigert wanted to throw out his guns, but Potts, even though in great pain, was afraid that they would be murdered if they gave up their weapons.

The sheriff waited as the pair continued to argue. He looked up at the sunset and admired its colors, then he heard a scream of terror followed by two rapid gunshots.

Manto appeared a few minutes later carrying extra weapons and stuffing money into his pants. "We take horses and saddles, rifles and food."

"Sure," Rudd said anxiously.

The Apache grinned and stared so hard at Rudd that he began to wonder if Manto might also be weighing the idea of killing him and then returning to his woman and wickiup a richer man.

"The gold can't be more than a few days ride from here, Manto. We'll find it soon."

The Apache kept staring at him, and finally Rudd had to look away. "Sheriff kill only one. Horse kill one. Manto kill four."

"So?"

"So Manto get four horses, saddles, and rifles. Sheriff can have two."

Rudd swallowed drily. He managed a smile and tried to put some bluster into his voice. "All right, I'll let you have the four outfits. But only because I got no use for 'em myself."

Manto grinned, but it wasn't a nice grin. Then, the Apache turned away and vanished into the fading light.

"He's going to kill me after we get that treasure," Rudd said to himself, "unless I kill him first."

SIXTEEN

"Look!" Clint said, reining Duke up sharply. "It seems that we're not alone after all."

Annie followed his eyes to a group of about ten men camped beside the Gila River. "Prospectors?"

"I don't know," Clint said. "But I've never seen prospectors idly hanging around together. Most of them are as secretive as squirrels. I'd say those boys are on to something other than panning gold."

"Do you think that they're after our Spanish gold?"

"What else?" Clint replied, starting to rein his horse back into the trees so that he and Annie could ride around the camp where the men had pitched their tents.

"Hello there!" a big, bearded man called, alerting the campsite to their presence.

"We could still ride away," Annie said nervously. "I don't like their looks."

"Neither do I," Clint said. "You stay right here, and I'll ride up to their camp and see what they're up to. If there's trouble, you ride out of here like a bat out of hell."

"And leave you? Not a chance."

"Listen," the Gunsmith argued, "if there's trouble, you'd be more of a worry to me than a help. So just do what I say, all right?"

"All right," Annie said reluctantly.

Clint managed a thin smile. "These are not gunfighters. They're rough and ready fellas, but I don't think they're looking to kill anyone."

"If they're after my father's Spanish gold, they're our enemies."

The Gunsmith thought it might be worth explaining to this young woman that the Spanish gold did not belong to her father or to her. Rather, a hidden treasure belonged to whoever was strong and smart enough to take it.

"Please be careful," she begged. "Clint, if anything happened to you . . ."

"It won't," he vowed, riding Duke forward, "but stay alert all the same."

Clint rode forward, a smile of greeting on his lips but his right hand very close to the butt of his gun. "Howdy," he called to the men who came forward to meet him.

The large, bearded man seemed to be the one in charge. "Howdy," he said, looking past Clint to Annie. "You don't need to leave your little woman back there by the trees, mister. We'd do her no harm."

"I'm sure that's true," the Gunsmith said easily, "but she's a mite bashful and we're just passing through."

"What are you doing way the hell up here in these mountains? It's too damn far from any town to be a pleasure ride."

"That's right. But it is pretty country."

"Pretty country?" A redheaded man with freckles chuckled. "Mister, you're about a hundred miles from civilization and the only thing pretty that I can see is your woman."

"Watch your tongue," Clint said in a soft warning. "I'll not have you gawking at her."

"Oh yeah?" the redheaded man said, his grin dying. "Well, I'll just stare at whatever I choose to stare at!"

"Jimmy," the leader said, "behave yourself. Can't you see that she's a lady, instead of a whore the likes of what you're always chasin' around after?"

The other men chuckled, but Clint was not reassured. He couldn't see any sign of prospecting, no sluice boxes, picks, or pans. Either these were outlaws hiding from some posse, or else they were looking for the Spanish gold, but their search had bogged down and they were trying to decide what to do next. Either way spelled big trouble.

"What are you fellas doing out here?" Clint asked matter-of-factly.

"Now whoa up, partner," the bearded man said, trying to sound friendly but not succeeding. "I asked you that question first."

"We're traveling over to Arizona."

"Why this far north and way the hell off in these high mountains?"

Clint thought hard and fast. "Actually," he said, trying to disarm them by looking sheepish, "we were only married last week in Silver City. So you see, we weren't interested in meeting a lot of folks because this is our honeymoon."

The big man's eyes rolled, and he gave a huge belly laugh which was taken up by everyone else present.

"Newlyweds, huh? Why don't you call your wife to come on over and we'll all congratulate her!"

"She's bashful," Clint said. "I think that we'll just ride on."

Clint started to rein Duke away, but the big man grabbed Duke's bridle. "Hang on, mister," he said, his voice taking on a low and nasty tone. "We just gave you and that pretty bride of yours a friendly invitation to share our company and now you're telling us that we aren't good enough for you?"

Clint knew that he was in a fix with the big man hanging on Duke's bridle, and so he decided to give talk one last chance before he went for his six-gun. "I sure didn't mean to insult you, mister, but me and my wife will be riding on. So I'm asking you to let go of my bridle."

The big man's eyes widened in mock concern. "And what'll happen if I don't?"

Clint knew that there was no sense in further conversation. His hand flashed to his six-gun, and it came up so fast that no one was prepared for the move.

"You want a hole blown in the top of your fat skull, or would you rather let go of my bridle and step back?" Clint asked in a quiet voice.

"Easy," the man said, his eyes round with fear. "Ain't no sense in any blood being shed."

"That's right," Clint said. "So loud and clear, let your friends know we have a peaceful understanding."

The big man nodded and then shouted, "Nobody goes for their gun! Everyone just step back easy and let this stranger ride away."

"Take your hand off my horse's bridle and come along until we get to the trees," Clint ordered. "And then we'll part on good terms. Understand?"

"Sure," the man said nervously. "Hell, mister, all me and the boys wanted to do was to show you a little hospitality. There was no cause for acting this way."

"Yes, there was," the Gunsmith countered. "When you put your hands on my horse, that was where a friendly invitation turned into a threat. Now come along."

With his six-gun trained on the man, Clint backed Duke up several yards and then ordered the bearded man to start walking toward Annie. Everything was going just fine until a movement caught the Gunsmith's eyes, and his head twisted around to see a lone hunter with a rifle and a pair of squirrels hanging over his shoulder. They stared at each other, and then the rifleman raised his weapon and fired.

Clint felt a bullet crease his skull. A red light exploded behind his eyes. In the next moment, he was on the ground, and the huge man was standing over him with a gun pointed at his face. Clint looked around at the mean-faced bunch that had formed a circle around him and realized he was in big, big trouble.

"Your bride and your black gelding both got away clean," the bearded man said. "She sure didn't show much loyalty to you, mister."

"I'm glad she ran," Clint said thickly. "She did exactly what I told her to do if there was gun trouble."

"Maybe she'll have a change of heart and come back," a man said hopefully. "Even if them boys that took out after her can't catch her on them two good horses."

"Not a chance," Clint said, trying to sit up but discovering that the effort made the top of his head feel like it was about to detonate. "Those horses will outrun anything you boys have to ride."

"We'll see."

Clint studied the hard ring of faces that surrounded him. "What do you want from me? I'll tell you straight out that I don't have much money."

"Give me what you got," the bearded man ordered, shoving his meaty fist downward.

Clint dug into his pockets and handed over a wad of bills.

"This here is a real nice six-gun," the big man said, turning Clint's Colt one way and then the other. "And from the way that you filled your hand, my guess is that you're a hired gunman."

"Your guess is wrong," Clint told him.

"Is it?"

"Sure. Like I said, my woman and I were just married."

"If you was up here honeymoonin', you'd be the worst kind of a fool and she'd be a saint. No, sir," the man said, "I think you're here for the same reason we're here and that's to find that Spanish gold. Ain't that right?"

"No."

The big man doubled up his fist and punched Clint alongside the jaw so hard that he sprawled across the dirt, tasting blood.

"Now, tell us the truth," the big man demanded, "or else I'll start to use my boots on you instead of my fists. And I guarantee that no mule kicks harder than Mike Lugas."

Clint's ears were ringing and his vision was blurred. He knew that it was pointless to resist or try to lie to this bunch while he was stunned and completely at their mercy.

"All right," he mumbled. "We were up here hunting for that Spanish gold."

"See?" Lugas shouted to those around him. "I knew that he was lying. Now mister, tell me what you know about that treasure and don't even think about lying to me or . . ."

"I know," Clint said, shaking his head, "or you'll boot my brains out."

"That's right."

Clint shook the cobwebs clear and worked his jaw to make sure that it wasn't broken. "I had a map, but it was stolen."

"By who?"

"The sheriff of Silver City."

"You talking about Ed Rudd?" someone asked.

"That's right. And there's little doubt that he and a few of his friends are on our back trail."

This news caused a flurry of comments from the rough group. One man snarled, "I never liked that bastard. If Rudd thinks he can horn in on this, he's got another thing coming."

Clint helped himself to his feet, realizing that he was still wobbly. He looked at the big man and said, "So what happens now?"

"That depends on what you remember about your map. Because right now, we're just plumb out of answers and patience. When you and that pretty lady arrived, we were taking a vote on whether to go back to Santa Fe or keep searching."

Clint took a deep breath. "I don't think I can help you much," he began, "because . . ."

Mike Lugas pistol-whipped him across the forehead so hard that Clint's legs broke at the knees and he spilled back to the earth. If it wasn't for his Stetson, the pistol would have laid his scalp open to the bone.

"I think," Lugas was saying, "that you need to have your memory refreshed. Boys, why don't you take this jasper over to the Gila River and see if a cold dunk will refresh his memory."

The men were only too happy to follow this suggestion. Clint felt himself being grabbed by several men and then dragged across the camp and into the water. He struggled but was powerless with so many having their cruel fun. Choking and swallowing water, he was held under the current until he thought for sure that he was going to drown.

"All right," Lugas said. "Haul him back up onto dry ground and let's see if he can remember things a little better."

Coughing and spluttering, Clint was tossed onto the grassy riverbank like a beached fish. For several moments, it was all he could do to replace the water in his lungs with pure, life-giving air.

"Now, mister gunfighter," Lugas said, balancing Clint's pistol in his hand, "one more time. Tell us where you and that woman of yours were heading to find the Spanish gold."

Clint looked up and knew that he was a dead man if he didn't come up with a good story fast.

SEVENTEEN

Annie had never been so scared in her life as when she'd seen the squirrel hunter throw his rifle to his shoulder and shoot Clint off his horse. Everything had happened so fast that Annie had been momentarily paralyzed with fear. Then, the squirrel hunter had started to spin around and shoot at her, but she'd finally reacted and sent her Arabian mare plunging into the forest.

Her escape had been equally terrifying. She'd just clung to her saddle horn and let the mare pick its way through the dense forest, ever climbing out of the Gila River canyon. Twice, Annie was almost ripped from her saddle by low-hanging branches. She would never have survived had she not been so afraid of being overtaken by the awful men camped far below.

It was only when her mare began to flag with exhaustion and Clint's black gelding pulled up to run neck and neck with her that Annie realized she had to slow down and think. Running blindly through these mountains was a good way to get yourself killed or hurt in a bad fall.

Annie did pull the Arabian mare in and then reached
out and collected Duke's trailing reins. She dismounted,
her legs weak with fear, and hurried into a sheltered
place where she had a commanding view of her back
trail. Pulling the Gunsmith's Winchester rifle from its
saddle scabbard, Annie levered a shell into its breech
and prepared for the worst. If men were coming after
her, then a few would die before they managed to either
kill or overwhelm her with their superior numbers.
Annie knew she could put up a good fight because Abe
Morton had insisted that his daughter ought to know
how to use a rifle.

Long minutes dragged by until the minutes
stretched into an hour. Annie's heartbeat gradu-
ally slowed, and she studied her surroundings. The
trail that her horse had chosen had been upward,
out of the deep river canyon. She was now situ-
ated in a thick pine forest characterized by huge
boulders. A stream trickled down from the higher
elevations and flowed to the river far below. Annie
moved over to the edge of the precipice and peered
down into the canyon. She watched and listened for
a long time but heard nothing except the jays in the
trees.

"They're not coming, or else I've lost them," Annie
said, taking comfort in the sound of her own voice.

For a few minutes, she was nearly overwhelmed
with relief. But then slowly relief gave way to the
realization that she would never be able to live with
herself if she left Clint at the mercy of that band of
murdering outlaws and cutthroats.

Annie collapsed on a rock and stared up at the sky
through a green canopy of pines. What was she going

to do now? How could she possibly rescue Clint without getting herself captured and killed? And what if he was already dead?

A thousand reasons why she should go on alone crossed Annie's troubled and fearful mind, but in the end, she knew that she had to go back and at least attempt to find out if Clint was dead or alive. And if he was alive, she had to save him somehow.

Annie waited another hour before she remounted and slowly retraced her back trail down into the canyon. When she saw the places that she had gone and the obstacles she had either ridden through or over, she was astonished.

"No wonder they weren't able to follow or keep up with me," she said out loud.

It was late in the day and the sun was already dipping behind the western peaks when Annie saw a plume of smoke rising from the Gila River camp, which she judged to be about a half mile away. Again, fear gripped her strongly, but she fought it off and tied the two weary horses.

"Don't whinny or make a fuss," she warned them, "or I'll be caught for sure."

The Arabian mare nuzzled her, and the big, black gelding sighed, acting glad to have a chance to rest and doze for at least a little while.

Annie took Clint's carbine and made sure that her own pistol was ready before she started back down the trail. Darkness fell quickly in the Mogollons and by the time she was near the Gila River, Annie could see the glow of the enemy's camp fire. Strangely, she felt at peace now that it was dark. If she were discovered, Annie was sure that she could escape into the black forest and hide, eventually making her way back to the horses which would carry her away to safety.

She would have this one chance to find out about Clint, and possibly to wait until after midnight and help him escape. If that resulted in failure, Annie knew that there would be no second chance.

The men were talking loudly, and when Annie crept down closer to their camp fire, she could hear them talking animatedly about her father's hidden Spanish gold.

"We'll find it," a man vowed. "With what that fella from Silver City told us and what we know ourselves, the treasure has to be buried downriver somewheres."

"Yeah, sure," another said, "but *where* downriver? Hell, the Gila runs all the way across Arizona to join the Colorado. We got to know *where* downriver or we're all just wastin' our time out here."

"Then go back to Santa Fe with your tail tucked between your legs," Lugas growled. "Don't make no never mind to the rest of us. I think our new friend here knows *exactly* where the gold is hidden. Don't you?"

Clint didn't reply. Annie took a sharp breath when she saw his battered face, one side of which was badly bruised and swollen. But he was very much alive, and although he was tied, hand and foot, Annie could see that he was fit enough to escape if she could cut his bonds.

"You hungry, mister?" Lugas said. "We're going to have a long day tomorrow hunting for that treasure. We don't want your mind to grow weak from hunger."

"I can't eat with my hands tied behind my back, and I'm not likely to escape with my ankles bound together," Clint said. "Cut the ropes and I'll have something to eat, but I'll be damned if I'm going to have one of you feeding me."

"Untie his hands," Lugas ordered. "Hell, there's ten of us, and he's in no shape to put up a fight. He can't run either, so what's the worry. Untie him."

Clint was untied at the wrists but with his ankles still bound he had to scoot over nearer to the fire.

"Here," Lugas said, tossing him a chunk of freshly roasted venison. "Wrap your innards around that."

Annie watched, feeling her heart begin to pound rapidly again as Clint ate, chewing his food slowly, as if his teeth ached. He seemed to pay no attention to the conversation around him, which centered on the Spanish gold, where it might be hidden and how much there would be to split among them. Some men even talked about the whiskey and the women they would buy with their newfound wealth.

Annie grew sleepy as the evening progressed. And one by one, the cutthroats began to climb into their bedrolls. Finally, only Clint and the bearded leader remained sitting and staring into the flames.

"You are a gunfighter, aren't you?" Mike Lugas said, looking sideways at his captive.

"No," Clint grunted. "I'm a gunsmith. I fix guns and do whatever I damn well please."

"And you were hunting the treasure," the big man said, "just like everyone else in these mountains."

When Clint didn't answer, Lugas frowned. "Is it true that the sheriff of Silver City is on your back trail along with some of his friends?"

"Yes."

"Why didn't you just lay an ambush?"

Clint shrugged. "Might be too many of them. Besides, I didn't want my wife to get hurt."

"Yeah," Lugas said, "that makes sense. She is quite a looker. She's probably on her way back to Silver City. Gonna find another man and forget all about you."

Clint lay back and closed his eyes. "I'm going to go to sleep now."

"If you try to escape, I'll make sure you die slow," Lugas promised. "Now roll over so I can tie your hands behind your back again."

"I won't try to escape."

"I don't believe you, mister. I saw the way you drew your six-gun, and I can tell that you've killed men before. I'd rather not join their ranks. Now, roll over and put your hands behind your back."

Clint had no choice but to comply. He felt his wrists being bound tightly, and when Lugas was satisfied, Clint rolled onto his side and tried to get comfortable. Maybe after Lugas went to sleep, he could figure out a way to get free and escape, but it wasn't going to be easy.

An hour passed before Clint was sure everyone had fallen asleep. He looked for the nearest knife so that he could cut himself free. He saw a knife sticking out of a hindquarter of roasted meat and was about to scoot over toward it when he saw Annie suddenly appear from the dark forest.

She held her finger to her lips as she tiptoed through the maze of snoring men until she reached his side. Annie already had a knife, and it cut through the Gunsmith's bonds as if they were cooked noodles.

He worked the circulation back into his fingers and then crept over and retrieved his six-gun from Lugas. Annie handed him his rifle. Motioning for Annie to lead them out of the camp, Clint slowly began to retreat. A few minutes later, they were running through the dark forest.

"Have you got both our horses?"

"Yes," she replied. "They're just up ahead."

"You're an angel!"

Annie flashed him a quick smile and kept running. When they finally reached their horses, the Gunsmith checked his cinch and jammed his rifle into its saddle scabbard.

"Let's ride," he said. "We'll lead them away from the river."

"What did you have to tell them?"

"I told them half-truths," the Gunsmith replied. "I'd taken such a banging that I didn't trust myself to completely make up some story about where we think the treasure is hidden."

"Will they follow us away from the Gila?"

"I think so," Clint replied. "Because until we blundered into their camp, they were at a dead end with no idea of where to search for that Spanish gold."

Annie nodded with understanding and then she followed the Gunsmith deeper into the high New Mexico mountains.

EIGHTEEN

Two days later, Clint and Annie lay flattened across a caprock ridge watching their back trail. They were both very tired and their horses were footsore, but there was excitement in their eyes.

"We've lost them," Clint finally said with conviction. "Lugas and his friends will never find their way up here."

"What will they do?"

"They'll wander around until they run out of patience or food, or both." Clint grinned. "When that happens, I expect that they'll either return to Santa Fe or else start following the Gila River in hopes of stumbling upon us digging up the buried treasure."

"It's not exactly on the Gila River," Annie said. "I mean . . . it's close, but my father said it was hidden about a half mile above the river."

This was news to the Gunsmith. "Are you sure?"

"Of course I am," Annie said, a little offended. "And I can see the last landmark."

"You can?" Clint stared at the young woman. "Well, point it out to me."

"It's this caprock."

Clint threw his head back and laughed at the cloudless sky. "And all this time, I thought that I was leading this hunt! But you were leading *me*."

"Not really," Annie said. "But I knew that this final landmark was somewhere off in this direction, so I was keeping a sharp eye out for it. And then, when you suggested that we actually ride up here so that our tracks would be almost impossible to follow on this caprock, I thought that it would be a lot of fun to surprise you."

"Well, you sure as hell have," Clint said. "So where is the treasure hidden?"

Annie drew her knees up to her chin. She gazed toward the Gila River, which appeared in the distance as little more than a short silver bar flanked by mountains. Annie shielded her eyes from the glare and said, "My father told me that you could see the river from here, but only a little segment of it between these barren peaks. They're important because when you look through them, that's where the treasure is hidden."

Clint estimated that the Gila River was a good six or seven miles away and that the tiny visible segment could not be more than a few hundred yards in length.

"Clint, can you find that little part of the river when we ride down there tomorrow?"

"Yeah," he said, staring hard at the distant band of silver, "I think so, though it won't be easy. What little of the river is visible from here looks to be bent to the north and back-dropped by the bald face of a cliff or rock slide."

"It's a cliff," she said with conviction. "And though it's too far to make out any details, it will have a cave."

"And that's where we'll find the Spanish gold? It sounds too easy."

"But it isn't. The cave is small and hidden," Annie explained. "My father said that it would be difficult to find, and that the trail leading up to it is very narrow and dangerous. That was one of the reasons why he always filled his pockets with coins before he left. Once, he barely escaped a fall that would have killed him."

Annie's eyes misted. "My father wasn't afraid of much, but he was afraid of heights. The cave is about seventy or eighty feet above the rocks below. One slip of the foot and . . . well, I think you understand."

"We did bring a couple of lariats," Clint said. "They will help. Are *you* afraid of heights?"

"I've never climbed the face of a cliff before," she replied. "Sitting up here like this doesn't scare me, but then, even though we are atop a range of mountains, there really isn't anyplace to fall."

"That's right," Clint said. "If it looks too bad, I'll climb up to the cave and toss the gold coins down so that you can gather and collect them."

"In what?"

"Our saddlebags."

"And if there are too many?"

Clint frowned. "If there are more coins than the saddlebags will hold, then we'll tie them up in our saddle blankets or bedrolls. Hell, Annie, I'll figure out some way to tie them onto the horses, even if it means we have to walk out of these mountains leading our horses."

"I almost hope that it comes to that."

"Do you have any idea exactly how much treasure there is waiting for us?"

"No," Annie replied. "My father said that many of the coins were scattered across the floor of the cave, covered by the dust and death of centuries. I guess that I might as well tell you that there are also a lot of human bones in that cave as well as some Spanish armor."

"Wow," Clint said, feeling his excitement build. "I'll bet there is one hell of an interesting story behind that gold, armor, and those bones. I wonder if the Spaniards were hiding in that cave from Indians."

"That's what my father always thought. He believed that the Spaniards were trapped and finally died of thirst in that cave along with their treasure."

"Be a hell of a way to die," Clint said with a troubled shake of his head. "You know, an ocean apart from your country and family, trapped like some animal in the wilderness, and forced to either leap to your death or die horribly of thirst. I can't help but feel sorry for those Spaniards. It must have been a bad end."

"My father used to make up stories about them. He even used to claim that their ghosts would visit him when he was camped near the cave." Annie frowned. "He felt haunted by those ghosts, and I think that was part of the reason why he drank so heavily. He told me that the ghosts didn't want anyone to take those Spanish coins. That's why he could only bring himself to take a dozen or so coins at a time. He was afraid that the ghosts would drive him mad if he took any more."

"That's a little crazy," Clint said in a quiet voice. "You don't believe in ghosts, do you?"

"I don't know what to believe. All I know is that my father said their ghosts followed him when he took their gold and they screamed at him in the night."

Clint looked away. He was not a superstitious man, and he didn't believe in ghosts, but neither would he have bet his life that they did not exist. All he knew for certain was that he'd never been visited by the ghost of a man he'd been forced to kill and that was damned important.

"I take it that you don't believe in ghosts," Annie said, studying him closely.

"Nope."

"Let's just hope that before this is all over, neither one of us has any reason to think differently about ghosts," Annie said with more than a little anxiety.

Clint stood and reached down to pull Annie up to her feet. "Let's just stop talking about ghosts and get moving. Time is wasting. If we hurry, we can reach that cave today."

"I won't spend a single night in it."

"All right," Clint agreed, trying hard to sound calm and relaxed when he really was getting excited about finally being so near the fabled treasure. "But let's find that river cliff while there is still light."

They led their horses down off the slippery caprock into the forest and tried to ride in as straight a line as possible toward the distant Gila River. However, they often came upon natural obstacles that either blocked their view of the river or else forced them to make wide detours. When this happened, they both grew tense and impatient.

"We're not going to make it to the river before dark," Clint said. "And I'm afraid that if we keep pushing these horses this hard, one of them may come up lame, and then we'll really be in a bad fix."

Annie glanced up at the dying sun. "Let's ride at least as long as we've got light and then camp. We can rise early tomorrow morning and find the cliff. Right?"

"Right," he answered, sensing her anxiety. "Don't worry, Annie, we haven't come this far to be denied."

They made their camp that night near a rushing mountain stream where there was feed for the horses. Clint felt confident enough about losing their pursuers that he dared to build a small camp fire nestled close in the rocks which would give off almost no light.

"They won't be able to see the smoke, but an Apache would be able to smell it from several miles away."

"Then maybe it isn't such a good idea," Annie said, crowding the flickering flames as the Gunsmith fanned life into them. "I mean, we could do without a fire."

"I suppose we could," Clint said. "But we're both half-starved, and the venison I have left is raw. I'm just not up to going hungry tonight, are you?"

"No," she admitted.

Clint cut strips of venison and laid them over willow sticks across the fire. The meat cooked quickly, and after they devoured it, the Gunsmith rekindled their little camp fire and cut more venison. They gorged until they were both satiated.

"A full belly and a good night's sleep will do us wonders," Clint said. "Tomorrow we'll both feel a whole lot better about this ghost business and about finding that cave and its ancient treasure."

"I'm sure you're right," Annie said, snuggling close. "If we can pull this off and escape out of these rugged mountains with our lives, it will be a small miracle."

"We'll find your father's Spanish gold and escape,"
Clint said. "I guarantee it."

Annie's eyelids drooped heavily. She tried but failed
to stifle a yawn. "I just want this to end. If it wasn't
that my father died trying to protect this secret so that
I could reap the rewards of his labor, I almost think I'd
be willing to forget the whole thing."

"Really?"

"Yes. This gold has caused so much death, and I'm
afraid that we haven't seen the end of it."

Clint thought about that for a moment. "Annie," he
finally said, "if we can find the gold tomorrow and leave
before dark, my hunch is that no one can overtake us
before we reach a bank in Silver City or Santa Fe."

"I'm thinking about Tucson," Annie said. "No one
would know us there, and we could buy a burro and
just ride into town and make our deposit. Once the
gold coins were deposited, we'd be safe, wouldn't we?"

"Sure. There are some big banks in Tucson. We could
even leave part of the money there and then take a
cashier's check and ride on to deposit it elsewhere."

"Now why would we do that?"

"Banks get robbed. If I were a bank robber, and I
knew that thousands of dollars worth of rare Spanish
coins were resting in one bank, I might be tempted to
try a holdup."

"I see your point."

"I was a lawman once," Clint told her, "and to be a
good one, you have to sort of train yourself to think
like an outlaw. You ask yourself, what would I do if I
wanted to rob a bank or a stagecoach or a train? How
would I pull it off?"

"How interesting," Annie said, yawning again.

Clint smiled. When the young woman's eyes finally closed and her chin dipped against her chest, he covered her with her bedroll, then resumed looking into the fire. Despite all his best intentions, Clint was thinking about the ghosts.

"Go to sleep and think about how you are going to finally get rich after all these years," he told himself.

Clint conjured up the image of a stack of gold coins and then he did fall into a dreamless sleep that lasted until dawn.

NINETEEN

Sheriff Rudd and the Apache tracker watched the camp's early morning excitement from a good vantage point. The sheriff turned to Manto and said, "What do you make of all that commotion?"

"They had the man we hunt and he got away," Manto said matter-of-factly. "They are very angry."

"They're a bunch of incompetent fools," Rudd said, his voice dripping with contempt. "I wonder what information they got out of Adams before he escaped."

Manto shrugged his shoulders.

"To hell with them," Rudd said. "We have to pick up the tracks of Adams and Morton's daughter. I got a hunch that we're getting close to that Spanish gold. We'd better find them before they dig it up and get too big a lead on us, or we'll wind up holding an empty bag."

The Apache slipped back deeper into the forest until he was well into cover, then he went to his horse and mounted it and headed off through the forest searching for tracks leading out of the river canyon. Sheriff

Rudd stayed quiet and followed at a healthy distance, keeping one eye on the Apache and the other over his shoulder in case the fools below should come boiling up their back trail.

It took Manto only about twenty minutes to pick up the trail, and he signaled with his hand to indicate that they should hurry. Rudd was only too happy to oblige. The last thing he wanted was to be overtaken by all those pissed-off fools down by the river who had allowed Adams to slip right through their fingers and run away with Annie.

The trail grew steep and winding. Manto was constantly on and off his horse, his black eyes missing nothing as the trail climbed higher and higher. Rudd could feel the tremble in his own legs as well as those of his horse. Neither of them were accustomed to this kind of punishment, and he guessed that they were now at least a couple of thousand feet higher than they would have been in Silver City. The altitude, the long hours on the trail, and the poor food were taking their toll on man and horse. Rudd knew he'd dropped a good ten pounds and his horse perhaps a hundred.

Two difficult hours later, they came to a halt before a huge, domed caprock that must have covered several hundred acres of mountaintop and ridge. The Apache studied every inch of the rock, which other than a few trees and boulders was completely bald and devoid of any sign of life.

"What are we waiting for now?" Rudd demanded with mounting impatience.

"No use to ride up there," the Apache said. "Better to walk around, search for tracks when they come off rock."

"I'll be damned if I am going to walk around this mountain when I've got a sound horse to ride."

"No matter. Manto walk," the Apache said, his dark eyes already scanning the ground in search of sign.

"But dammit, we could lose a couple hours!" the sheriff swore. "And what if we *can't* pick up their trail? I mean, it's damned clear that we're not tracking some ordinary yahoo. This Adams has proven he's a professional out here."

"Trail come off rock. No other way," the Apache said. "We find soon."

"You'd better," Rudd warned.

The Apache's head twisted around, and his hand went to the knife at his side. Rudd felt as if his heart was suddenly gripped by an iron fist. He gasped and stuttered, "I mean, I know how much you and your woman are counting on that gold."

Manto's lip curled. "Sheriff have big mouth and little heart. Someday, mouth kill him for damn sure."

Rudd gulped and tried to work up some bluster, but in truth he was so scared of the Apache that he couldn't even muster up a decent spit.

Manto cast him one final look of contempt and then began to lead his horse off to the west. He was not the kind to argue. He had already stated his intentions and what the sheriff did about that was none of his business. A man like Edward Rudd could either take his advice and follow, or else ignore his advice and go away. Manto didn't much care because his own mind was locked on this hard chase, which would end in a fight to the death for the Spanish gold.

"Dammit!" Rudd swore, booting his flagging horse after the Apache as they began to circle the immense caprock. The sheriff tried to guess exactly how much time they would lose before the Apache was able to pick up the trail again.

Manto did not allow himself to be hurried, and yet he covered ground with surprising quickness. His step was light and sure, his eyes missed nothing. Once, he pulled up short, and Rudd cried, "Did you find the tracks?"

But after a moment, Manto shook his head. "Bear," he said, eyes flicking off to a thick stand of timber less than a mile away.

They kept on searching until, late in the afternoon, they came upon the tracks. Manto's eyes followed them, and he could see the glint of the Gila River far, far away. He mounted his horse and set off at a trot.

"How far behind them are we?"

"Half day," the Apache replied, driving his horse down off the caprock and back into the trees. Manto did not have to strain his eyes any longer searching for tracks because he knew in his heart that the trail he followed would end at the Gila River.

Only fifteen miles back, Mike Lugas knew it was time to take control of his angry men. "Listen," he bellowed, "we can either tuck our tails between our legs and go back home, or we can ride on down this godforsaken river until we find that bastard and his woman digging up the Spanish gold."

Lugas waited a moment and then he demanded, "Now which is it going to be?"

"We find the gold!" a man shouted. "And then we kill them both and take the treasure for ourselves!"

Lugas was pleased as the others shouted in loud agreement. "All right then," he said. "Let's quit belly-achin' and start packing up and moving out."

It took the ten fortune hunters almost an hour to get everything ready and to catch up and saddle their horses. And even before the last man was astride his horse, he was spurring his mount into a jarring trot along the banks of the rushing Gila River.

TWENTY

When Clint rounded a bend in the Gila River and came face-to-face with the same cliff that he'd viewed earlier that day, he reined his horse up and grinned. "There it is, Annie. The place of golden fables."

Annie drew up beside him and gaped at the huge rock wall that towered overhead. "I never realized that the cliff was so big. Why, it must be a half mile wide."

"Wider, by my guess."

Clint studied the high, rocky face. The imposing cliff was well over a hundred feet tall, solid granite, and nearly perpendicular to the ground. The Gunsmith's first sweeping glance revealed no sign of any game trail or way to traverse its imposing face. There were, however, a number of vertical clefts. It seemed doubtful, but perhaps old Abe Morton had found a way to shinny up through them to a yet-to-be-revealed cave high above.

One thing was obvious; their two forty-foot lariats would be nearly worthless on such a cliff. And now, as the Gunsmith searched for a cave and saw nothing, he

lt his spirits plummet. Clint had not admitted it to
nnie, but he was no great shakes when it came to
caling heights and much preferred to keep his boots
n flat ground.

"Don't worry," she said, turning away from the cliff
nd trying to force a smile. "My father was far too old
o be good at climbing rocks. If he could find and reach
he cave, then so can we."

"Did he give you any idea exactly where on the face
f all that rock the Spaniards' cave is to be found?"

"Of course."

Clint waited, and when there was no response, he
aid, "Then where?"

"It will take me an hour or two to find the cave," she
aid, her voice mildly reproving. "Clint, you can't just
xpect me to ride up and point it out."

"Why not?"

"Because, if it were that easy, it would have been
liscovered by nearly everyone who followed this great
iver. Indians, mountain men and trappers, other pros-
ectors. Whatever treasure it held would have been
ooted long ago."

Clint supposed this was very much the truth. How-
ver, as the face of the massive cliff glinted sunlight
nto the river below, he wondered if the Spaniards who
ad died here could possibly have imagined how many
thers would follow their sad fate because of the gold
oins they had left behind so many centuries ago.

"Come on," Annie said, her eyes wide with excite-
ent. "Let's find that cave."

"I thought that you wanted to stay down below."

"I did," she admitted, "but seeing this has made me
ealize that I would always regret not visiting that

cave at least once. I'm sure you can understand that.

"I do. In fact, if you want to go up there instead of me and throw the coins down, I'll be happy to wait below."

Annie's laughing reply was high and nervous. It echoed off the canyon walls and raced the Gila River westward toward Arizona. When they came to the river, Annie glanced sideways at the Gunsmith. "Do you want to lead off across this river, or shall I?"

Clint studied the river. It was not deep, but it was swift. "Let's try to cross about a hundred yards down where it widens a little more and doesn't look to be so treacherous and deep."

Annie followed Clint downriver, and when they came to the place he had chosen to cross, she reined her Arabian mare in behind Duke and followed him across like a caboose on a train. The river was deeper than the Gunsmith had expected, and near its center Duke plunged into what was probably a channel and had to swim for about twenty yards before regaining his footing on the slippery rocks. With the Gunsmith's urging the black gelding humped the rest of the way across. The cliff seemed to be leaning directly overhead, as if waiting to bury them under tons of rock.

"Whew!" Annie called. "I'm glad that river isn't another three or four feet deep! As fast as it is, I think it would be easy to be swept away."

"You've got that right," Clint said, dismounting and removing his boots to empty water. "The river is deceptive. It looks shallow and that's a fooler."

Annie wasn't listening. She was staring up at the cliff. "My father never told me it was so steep and tall. I can't imagine him climbing up this monster."

"Neither can I," Clint said, remembering the old, andy-legged prospector. "Annie, are you sure that we ave the right cliff face?"

"I'm positive."

"All right," the Gunsmith replied, "then I'll unsaddle nd water the horses while you start looking for that ave. But don't go tromping around in the brush."

"Why not?"

"Rattlesnakes," Clint said. "I'm afraid that you'll be o busy craning your neck up that rock that you'll be n danger of stepping right on top of one."

Annie nodded in agreement. "Don't worry. I'll keep ne eye down and one eye up."

"Good."

Clint quickly unsaddled the horses. They were caked vith dried salty sweat, and he led them over to a sandy lace in the river and let them both roll in the water ike a couple of kids. It made him feel good to watch hem. When they had rolled and drank to their heart's ontent, he led both horses back to a place under the liff where they could graze. Since they weren't likely o swim the dangerous Gila, Clint let them graze on the iverbank grass. Both horses were showing their ribs, ind the Arabian in particular was looking skinny.

Clint moved in under the face of the cliff and laid out heir bedrolls, then eased down for a nap, placing his 3tetson over his eyes. He expected that Annie would let ›ut a shout when she finally spotted the cave, and until he did, there was no sense in dogging her heels.

He was so tired that he fell asleep almost at once and lid not awaken until Annie shook him. "Clint! Wake ıp! I think I've spotted it!"

The Gunsmith woke up fast. He knuckled sleep from

his eyes and struggled to his feet, noticing that the sun
was starting to sink into the west. "How far?"

"About a half mile downriver," she answered breath-
lessly. "I went upriver all the way to the end of the cliff
and didn't see anything. I remember that my father
said the cave was near a funny-looking rock stain.
Look up and you can see a lot of places where this
has happened."

"Yeah," he said, his eyes led by her pointing finger.
"I see what you mean."

"When I got to the wrong end of this cliff, I just
turned around and came marching back down. I almost
woke you up, but you were sleeping so peacefully that
I didn't have the heart so I hiked on downriver. That's
when I saw it."

"The cave?"

"No, the funny-looking stain."

"Oh." Clint scratched his head, unsure if he was
absorbing everything that Annie was saying. "But who
gives a hang about the stain? It's the cave that we're
after."

"I know! But the stain is *under* the cave."

"I see," he said, not sure if he was seeing at all.

"Come along!" she urged.

"I've got to pull on my boots. Go ahead and I'll catch
up in a minute."

Annie was so excited that she dashed off and yelled,
"Bring our ropes!"

Clint got his boots on and then collected their lariats. Almost as an afterthought, he also grabbed his
Winchester in the hope that he might be able to down
a nice buck. Their venison was about gone, and what
remained was starting to spoil with age.

He was still half-asleep and didn't catch up with Annie until she stopped, almost jumping up and down with impatience. "Hurry!"

"I'm hurrying," he groused. "But the Spanish treasure has been waiting for at least a couple of hundred years. I don't see what difference another five or ten minutes makes."

"Look!"

The Gunsmith craned his head back and stared. "What am I supposed to be looking at?"

"Follow that split in the rock up about eighty feet. See where that stain touches it?"

"You mean the one that looks like a smile?"

"Exactly!" Annie grabbed his arm. "That's got to be where the cave is located."

"I can't see anything," he complained.

"It's there," she insisted. "And look. There are lots of handholds in this split of the rock. Why, I wouldn't be surprised if you found a couple of gold coins in them."

"Annie," he said, not a bit sure that there was a cave up above. "I may be able to climb up that, but I'm pretty damn sure I won't be able to climb down."

"That's where those lariats will come in handy. You just tie one to something up there and . . . I know, you can wedge that rifle in between a pair of rocks and tie your rope to it."

"This is a good rifle!"

"It won't hurt it. Sling the rifle over your back, and it'll be perfect. It will be easy to climb up there! You could do it with your eyes closed."

Clint was not immune to Annie's excitement, although he thought the climb was more difficult than it first appeared. The schism in the rock which he would shinny up was about five feet wide and rough. He'd have to straddle space or else lean hard against one side of the cleft while trying to pick his footholds up the other.

"I can't believe that your father went up this, but if he could do it, then I can do it," Clint said, starting up the cleft in the rocks.

The going was fairly easy at first. Before the muscles in his legs started to cramp, Clint's assent was rapid. But about forty feet from the stain, his thighs began to knot, while both the handholds and footholds grew more scarce.

"What are you slowing down for?" Annie called from below. "You're only halfway up."

"There had better be a cave full of golden coins when I reach that stain," Clint warned, puffing and perspiring.

"There will be. I'm starting up now."

"No! If I should lose my footing and fall, I'd land right on top of you and we'd probably both be out of commission. You stand back and wait, Annie. If there is a cave, I'll lower a rope and pull you up."

"All right," she said, clearly disappointed.

Clint inched his way ever higher, anticipation and excitement driving him to the limit. He cursed old Abe Morton for not just tossing all the coins down and burying them at the foot of this cliff. But then, if the old man had done that, they might be gone by now or else all spent on whiskey.

"Clint, you're almost there!" Annie cried. "Just a few more yards."

"I know," he grunted, body drenched with sweat despite the high, cool mountain air.

Clint's leg muscles were shaking when he finally pulled himself up level with the black stain. Sweat was burning his eyes, and the granite had scraped his fingertips raw. He blinked away sweat, said a quick prayer, leaned out a little and looked toward the rock stain.

"I see it!" he shouted, crabbing up the last few feet to a narrow ledge that brought him to the mouth of a cave. The cave was set back from the lip so that it could not be seen from below, and the stain was caused by a small trickle of water that oozed out from another crevasse that angled in toward the cave from somewhere up above.

"What do you see?"

"I see a black hole. Annie, we're going to need some wood or something to make a torch. I'll lower the rope down and you bring them up. Hurry!"

Annie wasted no time in bundling some branches together that she knew would burn well. She also brought a stout branch, and when it was all tied together and slung over her shoulder, she called for the rope.

The Gunsmith tied their lariats end to end and threw the coil down to Annie. "Tie it around your waist and start climbing. If you slip, I'll stop your fall."

"You'd better use that rifle for a wedge, or I could pull you right over with me."

Annie was right. The Gunsmith tied his end of the rope around his Winchester and then wedged the rifle between the rocks. He braced his feet, took a coil of rope in his hands, and shouted, "All right, come on!"

The woman was so excited she almost flew up the cleft in the rocks. When Annie's face popped into sight, the Gunsmith motioned her forward. "Just take your time and don't hurry it," he warned. "We've got plenty of time."

Annie nodded, her face dirty and strained. She started across the ledge on her hands and knees. Once, when she glanced downward, Clint said, "Don't do that! It'll make you lose your nerve."

"It's already gone," Annie wheezed. "I must be out of my mind to be doing this, and so was my father and those poor Spaniards."

"Maybe they lowered themselves down from up above," Clint said. "I expect that might be easier. In fact, if you look off to your right, you can see a split in this cliff that might even lead to the top."

But Annie closed her eyes. "I need to catch my breath and stop my heart from beating so hard," she gasped. "I swear I must be crazy to be up here."

"Crazy or not, we're about to see that legendary Spanish treasure so many men have died over." Clint removed the brush and branch that Annie had brought up to make a torch and then dug into his shirt pocket until he found a match.

"Annie, I'll let you have the honor of leading the way to your father's treasure."

"Thanks, but no thanks. You lead the way, Clint. I might just faint when I see those old Spanish bones."

"All right," he told her. "I'll go first. Here goes."

Clint held up the crude torch and used his thumbnail to strike a match. The torch burned slowly until it caught a draft and then it flared up. Clint pushed it out at arm's length and said, "This thing isn't going to burn more than a few minutes so let's get in there, get the gold, and get the hell out."

"All right," she agreed. "I'm following right behind you."

Clint stepped forward, his heart in his throat. He had seen human skeletons before, but always in scattered fragments. Now, he was about to find them intact.

TWENTY-ONE

The Gunsmith recognized the dusty shapes of armor before he saw the skeletons. There were old, dented helmets, breastplates, even swords and shields. They were all piled up against one wall in disarray. There were several lances that had fallen over, and their shafts had rotted on the damp cave floor.

"Would you look at that?" Clint whispered, bending over to pick up one of the Spanish swords. It was surprisingly heavy and shorter than Clint would have expected. The blade was thick and double-edged, only about two feet long.

Clint tested the weapon's balance. "It's well made and designed, Annie."

"Put it down. We're not hear to loot armor, we want the Spanish gold."

Clint gently replaced the sword and moved around the relics of Spanish conquest and warfare. His crude torch spat and hissed, embers falling onto his arm and right hand. The Gunsmith advanced, eyes straining into the darkness. And then, he saw the skeletons and took in a sharp breath, his jaw dropping with shock.

In a voice that Clint did not recognize as his own, he croaked, "Did your father ever tell you how many Spaniards he found in this cave?"

"No."

"There were a bunch," Clint said, gulping and lifting the torch a little higher. "Looks to me like there must have been at least twenty-five. Perhaps as many as thirty."

The skeletons were lying randomly about everywhere, with no more order than rocks in a riverbed. All of the Spaniards had been dressed in heavy woolen and leather outfits, and their boots were torn open, black leather curling around twisted white bones. Silver and gold chains bearing heavy crucifixes were entwined in the rib cages or clutched in their bony hands. Several of the skulls wore rotted caps.

Clint observed that most of the Spaniards had expired while lying on their backs; their empty eye sockets were facing the roof of the cave. A few had died leaning up against the walls; their skeletons had broken in the middle and were bent forward with the weight of the quiet centuries. One man in particular caught and held the Gunsmith's attention because this Spaniard had obviously taken his own life. A wicked appearing dagger was deeply embedded between his ribs and still clenched by his hand. Its point was stained darkly by the blood of the poor man's heart.

"Oh," Annie cried. "I don't know if I can take this!"

"Steady."

"I'm trying," she whispered. "But Clint, can you imagine the torment these poor soldiers must have gone through as they waited for death?"

"I'm not at all sure that I really can," Clint said. "I'm surprised that the Indians didn't come up here and desecrate the bodies and take the armor."

"Maybe the Spaniards found this cave and decided to give up and die, knowing they didn't have the strength to walk back to Mexico. Maybe they'd already been in a terrible fight and had come badly wounded and seeking only to be left to face the end in peace. I'll bet they died one by one dreaming of their families in Spain."

"You reckon they came up from Mexico?"

"Yes," Annie said. "Mexico was under the rule of Spain since the time that Hernando Cortés conquered Montezuma and the Aztec people. That happened more than three hundred years ago."

"But the Spaniards weren't content to remain in Mexico." Clint knew something about the violent history of the Spaniards and of Old Mexico.

"No," Annie said, "their conquistadors marched up to find the Seven Lost Cities and their treasures of gold. They covered the Southwest in search of the lost cities they never could find. Most never made it back to Mexico City."

"They came looking for adventure and for gold," Clint said with a sad shake of his head. "Instead, these conquistadors found a lonely cave."

"I swear I can almost feel their ghosts swirling all around me," Annie said, throwing her eyes wildly around the inside of the cave. "I'm finding it hard even to breathe in here, Clint!"

"Stop it!" the Gunsmith ordered, whirling around and roughly shaking the young woman. "There's no ghosts in here, Annie, only bones, Spanish armor, weapons, and what we hope will be a fortune in gold coins."

Annie took a couple of deep, wheezing breaths. "I'm sorry. Let's find those coins."

"It's going to be all right," Clint said, gentling his voice and releasing her. "Just remember that your father found this cave and it cost him his life. Let's make sure that he didn't die in vain. Okay?"

"Yeah," Annie said in a small voice. "I'm fine. Let's get this over with."

Clint nodded and then grimly began to pick his way through the maze of skeletons. "I'm not leaving until I find those golden coins," he said out loud as if to convince himself that he dare not turn back even though his blood was running cold and there was a tremor in his voice.

The cave angled sharply to the right. Its floor was wet and slimy with moss. Rats skittered and scolded from the dark shadows, and the torch in Clint's hand began to flicker and grow dim.

"Where is our golden treasure?" he demanded, voice filling the cave.

And then he came upon a wooden box with rusted metal hinges that had been pried apart. The box's lid was missing, and when Clint lowered his torch, his eyes widened. The box was filled to overflowing with golden coins.

"Annie, we found it!" he shouted, dropping to his knees beside the old box.

She rushed to his side and buried her hands in the coins. Throwing back her head, she closed her eyes and whispered, "Thank you, Father!"

For several long moments, they just sat and stared at the treasure. In all his years out West, Clint had heard of thousands of buried treasures, many of them reputed to be left by the Spaniards. But he'd never known a single person to actually find such a treasure—until now.

"I can't believe this," he whispered, running his bloody fingertips back and forth across the cold coins and then squeezing them to make sure that they were real.

"Believe it," Annie said. "These coins *are* real. My father found them and he spent them. They're solid gold. They're the treasure of the ages."

"Why would the Spaniards bring gold to the New World when they were looking to find it?"

"I've read a little about them," Annie said. "They thought that the Indians they found would think of gold in the same way that they did, as being of great value. They intended to spend a little gold in the Indian villages in order to buy food, clothing, peace, and even directions to the Seven Lost Cities. It makes sense when you think about it."

"Yeah," he said, "I suppose it does. But the Indians they found didn't give a damn about gold."

"No," Annie said, "they did not. They wouldn't take gold in trade for corn, maize, and venison. When the Spaniards offered gold as a tribute, the Indian chiefs were often insulted. They could not understand why the conquistadors were so crazed for the yellow metal."

"I even feel a little crazed," Clint said, laughing nervously. "I've never had a lot of money. This is the stuff that people dream about but never really expect to find."

"But we *did* find it and it's ours," Annie said. "We're rich, Clint. We'll never have to think about money again."

He nodded and gazed at the box of Spanish coins, still pinching them as if they could not possibly be real. There were more than a hundred, and he could not even imagine their value.

Suddenly, however, an ember from the torch dropped on his hand and burned his flesh. Clint looked up and exclaimed, "Annie, the torch is going out! We've got to get this gold out of here! Take the torch!"

"What are we going to do? Oh, Clint, don't let us get caught way back here in the dark!"

Clint practically shoved the torch in Annie's face, and then he bent and grabbed the wooden box. It had rotted, but the Gunsmith thought that he could compensate for that by slipping his hands under the box and cradling it to his chest. If he could just get the damned thing to the mouth of the cave. . . .

The box was very heavy, and he did not raise it more than a foot when it crumbled in his hands, spilling gold coins across the floor of the cave.

"Damn!" Clint swore, tearing off his Stetson and blindly filling it with coins.

"We can use our boots!" Annie cried. "We can fill all four of them."

"Good idea, but how are you going to hold the torch—there it goes!"

The torch flickered and died, little branches glowing pale orange in the sudden darkness before dying away.

"Oh, Clint!" Annie screamed, throwing herself blindly into his arms. "I can't stand being in here without light!"

His Stetson spilled between them. The Gunsmith could feel Annie shaking violently in his arms.

"Listen," he said in as calm a voice as he could muster, "we've found the treasure. We're only fifty feet from light and fresh air, but we've *got* to get this gold out. Now you must get a firm hold of your senses."

"All right," she breathed, teeth chattering because of the cold and almost paralyzing fear.

"Let's take our boots off," Clint said, trying to keep his voice low and relaxed. "I've got a hat full of coins, and we'll fill all four boots. I think that will get us most of the treasure. I'll come back for the rest later."

"Anything you say."

Clint could hear the hysteria in Annie's voice and knew that she was very near the breaking point. She had probably heard about her father's ghosts for so many years that she actually believed they existed and being here without light was enough to push her over the edge of insanity. Clint knew that he had to get all the coins he could and then reach the mouth of the cave in a matter of seconds or there was the chilling possibility that Annie's mind might snap.

He worked feverishly to scoop the coins into his boots. There were still many gold coins left scattered about, and he spent a few frantic moments stuffing his pants and shirt pockets full of them. At last, he hooked his fingers through the pull loops and then gathered up his Stetson, which must have weighed thirty pounds.

"Let's go, Annie."

"I can still feel coins lying on the floor."

"Leave them. Grab your boots and then grab my coat. We're getting out of here right now."

Annie's hands swept back and forth a couple of last, desperate times and then she was grabbing the Gunsmith's coat and they began to shuffle back toward the bend in the cave.

"What if we step on the dead?" she asked in a small, frightened voice. "My God, Clint! What if we step on them and they break apart? If I hear their bones crunch underfoot, I'm afraid that I will . . ."

"Annie, we won't step on the Spaniards," he promised. "Just shuffle your feet across the ground. If we touch their remains, then we'll ease around."

Annie whimpered. Clint was sure that she was going to lose her mind if he did not get her out into the sunlight and fresh air in the next few minutes.

It seemed to take him hours to reach the dogleg, but when they turned it and started forward, the Gunsmith could see the light from outside the cave shining in at them. The light felt more precious than the gold that he carried.

Clint led Annie around the last few skeletons, past the dusty pile of Spanish armor, and out to the mouth of the cave where they spilled their treasure. They were both so emotionally drained by their experience that they collapsed on their pile of gold coins and lay feasting on the incredible beauty of a clear blue sky.

"We've done it," the Gunsmith whispered, his hands brushing back and forth across the golden coins. "Annie, we're rich!"

She hugged him tightly. "I can't ever go back in here, Clint. I *won't* go back in there!"

"You won't have to," he vowed. "Whatever treasure we lost in the darkness, we'll just leave for posterity. We've got more than we need. We'll leave this place as

soon as we catch our breath and gather our wits. We'll
lower ourselves down from this cliff, get on our horses
and ride. And this nightmare will finally be finished."

Annie raised her head. She was as pale as a marble
headstone and looked dazed. "We can go away and
never come back to this awful place?"

"Yes. If you want, we can even break camp and ride
across the river before dark. I don't know about you
but I'd like to be as far away from this cave as possible
by tonight."

Annie threw her arms around the Gunsmith's neck
and began to sob. Great, wrenching sobs that tore his
heart out. "It'll be all right," he assured her. "We've
done it, and we're getting out of here and never coming
back."

Annie wept with joy and relief until she could no
weep anymore. Then, she quieted and looked into his
eyes. "How are we going to get all these coins down to
our horses?"

Clint removed his coat. He cut short lengths out of
the lariat and tied off the arms and the neck of his
coat, then buttoned and filled it with the coins from
his Stetson and their boots. Working quickly because
there was less than an hour of daylight and he felt the
need to get away from this place, he tied the rope to
the coat. Satisfied, he came to his feet.

"I'm going to lower this down the face of the cliff.
Then we'll tie this end of the rope around my rifle
and wedge it between the rocks and get down ourselves."

"I can't tell you how happy that will make me feel."

"Me too," Clint admitted as he eased the heavy coat
over the edge and began to lower it down the face of

the cliff. It was hard work and his muscles corded with the effort.

The Gunsmith fed one rope out and was about to start lowering the second length when Annie cried, "Clint!"

"What?" he grunted through clenched teeth with legs planted, straining against the weight.

"They found us!"

Neck tendons bulging and face flushed with effort, Clint looked up and saw the riders appearing on the far side of the Gila River. "It's Mike Lugas and his boys!"

Annie covered her face and wept even harder as the riders from Santa Fe spotted them and began to gesture toward the face of the cliff.

"Annie, help me pull these coins back up!"

"Let them have it!" she cried with bitterness. "That gold is cursed!"

He glanced sideways at her in amazement. "No it isn't, Annie," he gritted. "It's gold, and it belongs to us. Now for God's sake, help me!"

But Annie violently shook her head and backed away.

Swearing and cussing, the Gunsmith began to pull the heavy treasure back up the face of the cliff. His arms and legs were on fire, and each time he reached down and tried to hoist the gold a few feet higher, the Gunsmith felt as if his back was going to break.

Mike Lugas and his boys threw themselves from their horses, grabbed their rifles, and opened fire from across the Gila River. The distance was about a hundred yards, and it took them a half dozen bullets to find their range.

"Annie!" the Gunsmith roared as bullets whistled around them. "If you don't help me pull this up, it's gone!"

"It's cursed!" she screamed. "Let them have it!"

"I'll be damned if . . ."

A bullet sliced the Gunsmith across his right forearm, and the pain was so sharp that he lost his grip on the rope. It burned through the palm of his left hand and then tore loose. Clint fell back under a hail of bullets, and he didn't have to hear the sound of his coat and the Spanish gold smashing into the rocks below.

"It's lost," he said. "We've lost it to them."

Annie crawled over to hug him around the neck. "It doesn't matter anymore. Let them have the gold. Clint, we're still alive, and maybe now they'll let us go!"

He pushed her back. "Annie, your father died for this treasure, and I've just gone through hell. Do you really think that I can sit by and let Mike Lugas and his cutthroats claim what is rightfully ours?"

"What choice do we have? Do you want *our* bones to join those inside? This is a place of death! It's cursed, and we'll never get out alive if we don't let everything go."

He swallowed noisily. He wanted to argue but could not deny that he felt in his own bones that the girl was right.

"All right," Clint said. "We'll see if we can trade those coins for our lives."

She nodded rapidly and even managed a hopeful smile. "Do you think they'll do that?"

"No," he admitted. "I doubt that there is anything I can say that will convince those greedy bastards that most of the gold was in that coat. They'll think that the treasure is far greater, and they won't be satisfied until we are dead and they've been inside this cave to search it for themselves."

"Then we are lost," Annie whispered, her voice breaking as she clung to him as if she were drowning in the river far, far below.

TWENTY-TWO

The Gunsmith eased up to peer over the lip of the cave as a hail of bullets screamed overhead. He poked his rifle out into space and took aim on Mike Lugas's chest, then slowly pulled the trigger. The rifle barked, and his shot echoed up and down the canyon walls even as Lugas slapped his heart and fell into the Gila River, which swiftly carried his body away.

"One down and nine to go," Clint said, ducking his head as another swarm of bullets passed over him to ricochet off the interior of the cave.

Clint waited about five seconds, and then he spotted the cruel man with the red beard. A tight smile formed on the Gunsmith's face, and he drilled the man in the gut. The red-haired man screamed and toppled over, feet beating in the dust.

"Two down and eight to go," Clint said, easing back and glancing sideways at Annie. "Are you all right?"

"I don't know," she whispered. "How many bullets do you have left in that Winchester?"

"Enough, if I don't waste too many," Clint replied.

"But I doubt even this crowd is going to be stupid enough to give me another good target."

"And they're too greedy to run."

"That goes without saying," Clint answered, easing forward to look down and across the river. Sure enough, the men from Santa Fe had taken cover. Clint waited patiently until he finally had a target, then he took his time and quietly sent a bullet through the crown of a man's hat.

"Three down and seven to go," he said with satisfaction.

"What are we going to do?" Annie asked. "We can't survive up here any better than the Spaniards."

"We've got water. And we might be able to climb up to the top along that same cleft in the rock that brought us up this far."

"Do you think so?"

"I don't know," Clint said. "But when I get to starving, my aim gets a little shaky, and I'm not about to let that happen."

"Why don't you see if they would let us go if we let them keep the gold we dropped?"

"I guess it's worth a try," he said, "but I still think they'll try and starve us out and then come up to make sure we aren't hoarding a bunch more."

"We could buy ourselves time," Annie said. "After all, they can't reach the gold as long as we're up here."

"Don't be too sure of that," Clint said. "There isn't going to be much of a moon tonight, and I'd have to hang way out into the air in order to shoot straight down on them. The truth is, I'll be a better target than they will after dark."

"I didn't think about that," Annie said. "But that just

makes it all the more necessary that we try to come to a truce."

Clint supposed that the woman was right. "Give me that stout branch you brought up here," he said, easing back into the cave and removing the gold coins stuffed into his shirt pockets before taking off the shirt itself. "I'll tie this on and wave it over the side to show we want to talk peace."

"Good!" Annie quickly found the branch. "Why, you must have stuffed twenty gold coins in your shirt pockets."

"Count 'em."

"Twenty-two," she said.

"I've got about that many crammed into my pants pockets," he said. "And I mean to collect whatever we left back in that cave. Annie, I'm not about to come through all this broke."

She nodded with understanding and helped him fasten his shirt to the pole, saying, "That should stay attached."

Clint slowly pushed the shirt and pole out into the air. Someone took a pot shot at the truce flag, but that was not surprising, there was always at least one trigger-happy fool in every crowd.

"Let's talk!" Clint shouted.

"Why should we?" a voice floated up from across the river. "You're meat!"

"We've got food and water!" Clint yelled. "We can stay up here for weeks."

The men didn't have an answer for that. Clint eased the flag of truce back into the cave, figuring that the seven were probably arguing over what to do next.

Finally, one of the men from Santa Fe yelled, "If you

come down, we'll let you and your bride go free, no questions asked."

"You're crazy!" Clint shouted. "No deal!"

One of them fired up at the cliff. A bullet sprayed shards of granite as the Gunsmith shielded Annie with his body.

"What are we going to do now?" Annie asked.

"Wait until dark and then see if we can climb out of here. There might even be a way back through this cave."

Annie's eyes widened with fear. "I can't go back in there! I'd rather die!"

"No you wouldn't," he said roughly. "And I'm not about to let that happen."

The Gunsmith replaced his hat on his head. He took his shirt and wrapped it around the edge of the stout pole. "I'm going back inside to look for a back way out of that cave and to collect whatever coins we left on the floor. Are you coming?"

"I can't," she whispered, tears springing to her eyes. "I just can't!"

"All right," Clint said gently. "Don't worry. I won't be long. Just stay down close to the floor and you'll be all right. The chances of a bullet ricocheting back in this direction from somewhere in the cave are nonexistent."

"Please don't stay more than a few minutes."

"Annie, I have to find out if there is an escape through the rear of that cave. A passage up to the top that we can take. If there isn't, we have no choice but to crab our way up the crevice and onto the top. And that might not be too healthy."

Clint left her then. He touched a match to his second makeshift torch, knowing the shirt would burn quickly but hoping that perhaps the stout branch would continue to burn and give him a little more time to explore.

This time the Gunsmith barely glanced at the armor or the skeletons. He hurried back to the gold, thought to collect it, and then rejected the thought, knowing he needed to inspect the cave to its ending.

Unfortunately, this took less than two minutes. He found three more skeletons and what looked to be a banner affixed to a pole before he came to the cave's end. He held the torch up and watched water seep through the rock wall into a small pool which then fed out onto the floor of the cave. He also saw the red, winking eyes of dozens of rats.

"Sorry to disturb you boys," he told them.

A few minutes later, he knelt and collected the rest of the Spanish coins in his hat, counting as he scooped them up. There were eighty-four, and he knew that he would still be very well-fixed if he and Annie could figure a way to escape this death cave.

"Thank God you're back!" Annie said. "I was getting so worried."

"Any more action from out there?"

"No, and the sun is going down."

"Good," Clint said, showing her the coins he'd collected. "Take off your blouse and tie these up in a bundle that we can carry out of here."

"What?"

"Either that or your riding skirt. Doesn't matter to me. I've already sacrificed my shirt for the torch."

"But you're a man. A shirt isn't that important."

"Look," he said patiently, "I lost my coat over the

side. Remember? Then I burned my damned shirt up as a torch while I hunted for a back exit out of this mess. The only thing I've got left are my boots and my pants, and I'm not giving up either. So off with your blouse."

"You're not as nice as I thought you were," Annie pouted as she removed her blouse. She wasn't wearing anything underneath the blouse, and the Gunsmith couldn't help but notice that her nipples were hard, probably because the air was cold.

Clint glanced up at the fading light. The men from Santa Fe were being extremely cautious, and he couldn't see any of them, but he knew they would be coming to collect the treasure of coins that he and Annie had accidently spilled a few hours earlier. To hell with them, he thought. It galled him to think that those men would get all that Spanish gold, but there was no sense in worrying about what he could no longer control. The smart thing to do was to try and climb up and off the face of this cliff while they were still strong and able.

"If we can get away," Annie said, "we'll still have over a hundred coins. We'll still be rich."

"Not rich, but comfortable."

"Whatever." Annie pressed close to the Gunsmith. "Wrap your arms around me, I'm cold."

"That's about to change," he said. "Because, in just a few minutes, we're going to start climbing."

"What then?"

"I'm going to find you and our gold a safe hiding place, and then I'll get back down and collect our horses. We're not about to walk out of these mountains. We're in too deep and . . ."

Clint was about to say more, but there was a sudden volley of gunfire. It was dusk, and he could see muzzle flame and hear men shouting.

"What's going on?" Annie cried with alarm as they both tried to penetrate the darkness and see what was happening on the far side of the river.

"They might be fighting among themselves," Clint said. "But I think they're being shot by Rudd and his friends."

"Then we've got even more trouble."

"Not necessarily. They might all be killing each other, which would be just fine."

At last, the gunfire ended. Clint heard a death scream after about an hour and then nothing more. He waited until a pale slice of moon appeared, then he coiled their ropes, collected Annie's blouse stuffed with gold, and said, "Let's go, Annie. We're as good as dead unless we get off the face of this cliff tonight."

Annie understood and believed. "What happens now?"

"We tie this rope around each other, leaving about ten feet in between, and then we climb."

And that's what they did. The climb wasn't as difficult as the Gunsmith had imagined, and the darkness gave them the added advantage of not being able to see how far they could plummet to their deaths. It took them less than an hour to climb up the deep cleft in the rock, and when they reached the top, they lay panting and gazing up at the stars.

"We did it," the Gunsmith said. "Annie, we did it!"

He helped Annie to his feet and got his bearings. "Now," he said, "we find you a hiding place and—"

The Apache tracker jumped out at them both, his

knife glinting in the starlight. Clint's hand flashed for his gun, but Manto was already on him. The Gunsmith had to forget about his pistol and grab the Apache's wrist to keep the knife from driving deep into his gut.

"Clint!" Annie screamed as the Gunsmith and the Indian rolled over and over in a life and death struggle.

Manto was extremely powerful. It took the Gunsmith only a moment to realize that he could not match the Indian's strength and that he was going to die unless something drastic happened.

"Annie, help!" he shouted as they rolled up to the edge of the cliff, Manto on top, pressing his knife downward toward the Gunsmith's throat.

She grabbed a rock. Rushing forward, Annie stumbled in her haste and spilled to her knees. She crawled forward, and the Apache's head twisted to glare at her. Annie's breath caught in her throat, and she swung at the Apache's face. The rock struck Manto, and he grunted with pain.

"Hit him again!" Clint shouted.

Annie bashed the Apache a second time, and Manto finally sagged. The Gunsmith bucked, throwing the Apache over the edge. Arms flailing wildly, Manto somehow managed to grab the edge of the cliff and dangle high above the Gila River canyon.

"Clint!" Annie shouted, dropping her rock and rushing to his aid.

The Gunsmith rolled to his hands and knees. In the faint moonlight, he could hear the Apache's breath coming fast as he tried to pull himself to safety. The Gunsmith picked up the Indian's knife and pressed the edge down across Manto's bloodless, straining fingers.

The Apache gazed defiantly up at Clint, who said, "What happened down on the river?"

"Go to hell!"

The Gunsmith leaned on the blade and watched as it cut into the Apache's fingers. "One more time if you want to live. What happened?"

"Sheriff Rudd and the others dead! All dead except Manto!"

"Did you kill the sheriff?"

Manto glared up at him, and Clint knew in an instant that the Apache had indeed killed Sheriff Rudd.

"I'll make you a deal," Clint said, knowing he might be about to make a fatal mistake. "If you let us get our horses then ride out of here with whatever gold we carry, you can have the rest. You'll find it scattered all over the base of this cliff. Do we have a deal?"

Manto spit up into his face.

"I'm sorry you made such a bad choice," Clint said. "Because now Annie and I will have to spend all of the gold."

And with that, the Gunsmith leaned on the knife, and the Apache went hurdling out into space.

"Clint!" Annie screamed. "How could you do that?"

The Gunsmith climbed to his feet, wiped his face, and said, "Because he couldn't lie or go against his nature. He'd have killed us and taken all the gold for himself. We'd have never gotten out of these mountains alive."

"Are you sure?"

"Yes," Clint replied. "Just as sure as I am that everyone on the far side of the Gila River is dead, including the late sheriff of Silver City."

Annie pressed herself tightly to the Gunsmith, and

he felt her shiver with cold. "Come on," he said, "let's get down to our horses and get you wrapped up in something warm. In the morning, I'll do the burying and you can collect your father's treasure. If we work hard, we can be out of this death canyon by noon."

"That's all I want," she said. "Just you and to get away from here, *never* to return."

"And the gold," he added with grim satisfaction, "our legendary Spanish gold."

J. R. ROBERTS

THE

GUNSMITH